Montana
★ MAVERICKS

**Stories of family and romance
beneath the Big Sky!**

**"That is the skimpiest bathing suit I've ever
seen," Pierce told Chelsea as she rose out of
the icy water of the lake.**

She looked at her two-piece suit. It was cut high
on the legs, as all of them were. "Surely not,"
she said airily.

Uh-oh, wrong thing to say. He looked as if he
would like to choke her.

"That outfit might be modest for the city, but
around here, folks dress more circumspectly."

Chelsea couldn't help it. She burst out laughing.
"I'm sorry. It's just that you don't sound at
all like the Pierce Dalton who dared me to go
skinny dipping in the pool at my apartment
building at three o'clock on a January morning."

"I'm not here to discuss the past," he informed
her. "If the guys working here see you like that,
they'll take it as an open invitation to visit. I
won't have them distracted by a siren from the
city."

Chelsea rubbed the end of the towel over her
dripping hair. "You'd better watch yourself, too,
Pierce. City sirens are hard to resist."

Montana
★MAVERICKS

LAURIE PAIGE

Her Montana Man

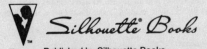

Silhouette Books

Published by Silhouette Books
America's Publisher of Contemporary Romance

Special thanks and acknowledgment to Laurie Paige
for her contribution to the Montana Mavericks series.

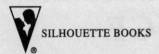

SILHOUETTE BOOKS

ISBN-13: 978-0-373-36237-0

Recycling programs
for this product may
not exist in your area.

HER MONTANA MAN

www.Harlequin.com

Printed in U.S.A.

LAURIE PAIGE

"One of the nicest things about writing romances is researching locales, careers and ideas. In the interest of authenticity, most writers will try anything...once." Along with her writing adventures, Laurie has been a NASA engineer, a past president of the Romance Writers of America, a mother and a grandmother. She was twice a RITA® Award finalist for Best Traditional Romance and has won awards from *RT Book Reviews* for Best Silhouette Special Edition and Best Silhouette, in addition to appearing on the *USA TODAY* bestseller list. Recently resettled in Northern California, Laurie is looking forward to whatever experiences her next novel brings.

To Bobby and Melba,
for all the adventures in Montana.

Chapter One

Chelsea Kearns stripped the surgical gloves from her hands and tossed them in the Contaminated Waste Disposal bin. In the locker room she showered, then dressed in street clothing of khaki slacks and a cotton shirt of cool, mint green.

Once outside the hospital, which housed the county morgue, she breathed deeply several times before unlocking her car from the passenger side, opening both doors and letting the accumulated heat escape.

Here in the Beartooth Mountains of Montana just north of Yellowstone National Park, summers were usually pleasant—low eighties during the day, forties at night. The temperature on the digital display at the bank proclaimed the temperature to be ninety-three.

"This heat is terrible. It must be global warming," a passerby said to her companion as they strolled past Chelsea. "The government should do something."

"Maybe we'll have a thundershower later this afternoon," the companion said in a soothing voice.

The first woman grimaced. "Those only bring lightning and forest fires at this time of the year."

Chelsea sympathized with the ill-humored woman. She felt out of sorts herself. The bank clock indicated it was well past the noon hour on Wednesday, July third.

She'd eaten a quick breakfast at five-thirty, but she wasn't hungry. She never was after a morning spent in the morgue, doing her job as a medical examiner. The autopsy had disclosed information that was going to shock most people in the town of Rumor, located twenty miles from here.

Tossing her purse onto the passenger seat, she reluctantly followed it inside the hot car and started the engine. She turned the air conditioner on full blast and aimed the vents directly at her face.

Leaving Whitehorn, she followed the highway to the turnoff that would take her to Rumor, Montana, and the lakeside cottage where she would be staying for the next three weeks. This first week she had to work, but after that she had two solid weeks of vacation.

Ah, bliss.

However, before the fun began she had bad news to report to the deputy sheriff in charge of the investigation. The autopsy she'd performed indicated murder, not suicide; although, the perpetrator had tried to make it look that way.

The absence of powder burns precluded a self-inflicted shot, or else the victim would have had to have held the weapon with her toes in order to inflict a wound in her left temple at a sufficient distance. Besides all that, the angle of entry of the projectile was all wrong for suicide.

Chelsea sighed. This was going to be a tough case. She could feel it in her bones. The trial, assuming they caught the guy who did it, would be time consuming. She'd have to come down from Billings, an hour's drive each way, and testify about her findings. The defense attorney would try to prove she didn't know what she was talking about.

She sighed again. There was also the complication of Pierce Dalton—successful businessman, mayor of Rumor where the murder had been committed, brother to her best friend, Kelly, and…former lover.

Her life, which had seemed calm and sensible when she'd accepted the position as medical examiner in Billings, suddenly seemed complicated.

Maybe she should have stayed in Chicago. She'd been busy but lonely in the city, she admitted. And she'd missed the mountains. Had she also wanted to see Pierce again? She didn't have an answer for that.

Arriving in town, she slowed to the requisite thirty-five miles per hour for the short drive down Main

Street, then turned right onto Blue Spruce Road and right again onto the lane that took her to a modern cottage set among towering evergreen trees next to a jewel of a lake.

With a deck built out at the edge of a tiny cove, the place was as enchanting as a scene in a fairy tale.

Grabbing her purse, which held her recorder and the notes dictated that morning, she went in and changed to shorts, a comfortable T-shirt and flip-flops. On the deck, with a tall glass of iced tea and her handy laptop computer, she began her formal report.

Sometime later, the sound of tires on the gravel lane interrupted her concentration. She heard a car door slam, then silence. She waited until a knock sounded on the cabin door before calling out, "I'm on the deck."

A male figure appeared at the corner of the cabin. Dressed in jeans and a polo shirt, his stride long and assured, the visitor exuded power and authority.

She instantly recognized the sandy-blond hair and six-two frame of her long-ago lover. Pierce was a man with a commanding presence. She hadn't been surprised when Kelly had told her Pierce was now mayor of the town.

The jagged edge of remembered hurt plucked at her heart, a never-forgotten melody of love and wonder and, ultimately, rejection. Pierce had made it clear he was not a settling-down kind of man the last time she'd seen him.

"Hello, Pierce," she managed to say in a quiet manner.

Two years older than she was, at thirty-six he looked trim and fit, a prime male specimen with his blue eyes and handsome, somewhat rugged features. He'd always reminded her of the mountains—strong and solid and inspiring.

It had been eight years since she'd last seen him. They'd parted one stormy April night, two months before she graduated medical school. So many dreams ago.

He ignored the three steps and leaped to the deck in a single, graceful bound. "Chelsea," he said, acknowledging her greeting. He didn't smile.

So what had she expected—that he would gaze soulfully into her eyes and declare he'd never gotten over his love for her and that she must marry him at once so they could live happily ever after?

Dream on, she thought, and would have laughed had it been the least funny.

"You have a wonderful place over there," she said, indicating the resort, the lake and the idyllic setting.

He nodded, his mind obviously not on the scenery. "What did you find out?"

Blunt and to the point. She'd wondered how he would react to her being here—on his turf, so to speak—so now she knew. She could be all business, too.

"I'm preparing a report for the deputy," she told him with a polite smile. "He'll have it Friday morning."

"I want it now."

She started to make a smart remark, but, seeing the concern in his eyes, she refrained. This was his hometown and he was the mayor. Murder was serious business.

"You'd better have a seat," she advised. "Would you like a glass of iced tea?" She'd finished her own glass while working on the report.

Impatience flickered over his face and was gone. He nodded and settled in the deck chair facing the lake.

She quickly prepared the refreshing drinks, then, after a struggle with herself about playing the polite hostess, arranged a tray of crackers, cheese, veggies and dip and carried them outside.

"Thanks," he said, taking the glass she indicated and pulling a table between their two chairs so she could set the tray down.

When she was seated, he leaned forward, his blue eyes focused intently on her. It would have been exciting, except she knew he was interested only in her information.

"The victim died of a gunshot wound to the head," she told him. "The bullet entered the left temple and ricocheted in the skull without exiting, inflicting severe brain damage and instant death."

"I can't believe she'd commit suicide."

Chelsea gave him a level perusal. "She didn't."

"She didn't?" he echoed, his eyes hot blue lasers as he glared at her.

"She was semiconscious from a blow to the back of the head. Prior to that, she'd been slapped hard enough to leave a bruise. From scrapes on her elbow and knees, she probably fell to the floor. She was then placed in a chair and shot from a distance of three or four feet. Panicking, the perp decided he'd better make it look like suicide."

"Why panic and why a *he?*"

Chelsea considered the evidence before replying. "The victim was hit hard enough to knock her unconscious or nearly so—"

"Harriet," he broke in. "Her name was Harriet Martel."

Chelsea kept a bland expression. She'd learned during her five years of pathology training and three years on the job to keep an emotional distance from those who'd died by violence; otherwise, her job would become unbearable.

"From the deputy sheriff's report, Miss Martel was knocked to the floor, then lifted, not dragged, to the chair. Both facts indicate strength. If you're looking for a female perp, she's strong as an ox."

He gave a grunt that could have indicated agreement, skepticism or any number of things. "Why did he panic?"

"His anger cooled after he killed her. He realized he needed to make it look like suicide and that someone might have heard the shot. He wanted to get away, so he was hasty in setting up the scene. He wiped the gun, then pressed her fingers into position around it."

Pierce frowned at her. "The gun was found on the floor beside the chair."

"Planted to look as if she dropped it after the shot."

Chelsea watched a couple push off from a dock across the lake. Cabins nestled among the trees over there. Pierce had started from scratch and made a huge fortune in real estate and recreational activities for tourists, so his sister had said. Good for him.

"However," she continued, pulling her gaze from the happy couple, whose laughter she could hear drifting over the water like an echo from happier times in her own past, "he messed up. Suicide victims usually retain the gun in a death grip that's almost impossible to break."

Pierce was quick on the uptake. "Usually?"

"Yes. That's the first thing you look for in a suspected suicide. But it doesn't always happen, so I examined the weapon. From the fingerprint evidence, Miss Martel didn't exert enough force on the gun to pull the trigger, much less hold it in place to kill herself. There were no powder burns, either."

"So the gun had to be held at least a few feet from her," he murmured, frowning as he considered this fact.

Chelsea nodded and lifted her glass. The tea was cold and tart from the generous squeeze of lemon she'd put in. She hadn't added any lemon to his glass on the assumption he still liked it with one spoon of sugar and no lemon.

Eight years was a long time, she reflected. Perhaps his tastes had changed. However, he didn't say anything as he took a long drink, then rubbed at the condensation on the glass while he thought.

She continued with her conclusions about the crime. "I think the killer didn't decide to shoot her until he placed her in the chair. They'd been quarreling. Perhaps she'd hit him first. Now she was vulnerable, in his power. He needed to get rid of her, to keep her quiet—"

"Why?" Pierce demanded.

Chelsea met his gaze. "The victim…Miss Martel… was pregnant. About four months, I would say."

"She couldn't have been," he said. "She was an old maid, the town librarian, for Pete's sake. She didn't date anyone."

"Maybe not," Chelsea said coolly. "But she was certainly having an affair. I'd look for a married man with a lot to lose if the scandal got out, someone in a prominent position in town, maybe someone on the city council."

"Yeah, right," Pierce said in a snarl, rising to his feet and looming over her. "The council is composed of a retired rancher, a high school coach at least fifteen years younger than Harriet, plus three women. That's certainly a bunch of likely suspects."

"The motive was conjecture on my part," she readily admitted. "Your investigators will have to ferret out fact from fiction. I'd start with the woman's secret life."

Lips that had once kissed her thousands of times thinned to a straight line. "What about your life?" he asked in a soft tone that sent shivers along her neck.

She met his gaze that contained no signs of welcome for her in it. "What about it?"

"Why did you come back to Montana?"

Smiling slightly, she answered truthfully, "I always loved the mountains."

He studied her for another ten seconds, then walked off, disappearing around the house. A minute later she heard his vehicle on the gravel as he left.

Peering through the trees at another house no more than a football field away, she wondered why he'd bothered to drive. He lived over there, just across the creek that fed icy mountain water into the lake. Kelly had said it was a marvelous house, meant for a family.

Chelsea sighed as gloom settled over her. An innocent life had been snuffed out when the librarian was killed. The violence of deliberately inflicted death disturbed her. The person hadn't cared about the child at all.

Laying a hand over her abdomen, she recalled her own plans. She'd assumed she would have a home and family. She'd thought Pierce would be the man in her life. Instead she had an apartment and no husband or children in sight.

Some things were never meant to be. She managed a smile at life's ironies, reviewed the report and went inside before dark.

"Chelsea, I can't believe you're here!" Kelly Dalton Brenner threw her arms around her best friend and gave her a bone-shattering hug late Thursday afternoon. "I'm so glad."

Chelsea returned Kelly's bear hug. They'd met in medical school and had been assigned the same cadaver to autopsy. The horrifying—at the time—experience had made them friends forever. Now Kelly was a family physician with a busy practice in a large county with few doctors. Her husband, Jim Brenner, was a hunting and fishing guide and owned the local sporting goods store.

"I'm glad, too. This is a beautiful place."

Kelly tucked a flyaway strand of hair behind her ear. "Bet you couldn't sleep—not enough noise. All the city dudes complain about that the first couple of nights."

"Actually, there was too much racket. Those crickets and tree frogs kept up a chorus all night. One of them was definitely off tune."

"Come on. It's nearly time to eat." Kelly pointed toward the house barely visible through the trees lining the creek.

"Are you sure it's okay for me to come?" Chelsea hated the uncertainty that plagued her. With it was an undefined sense of excitement brought on by more than the prospect of a Fourth of July picnic and fireworks by the lake.

"Of course. The whole town is invited."

That news didn't make her feel more comfortable. She was hesitant to see Pierce again. Perhaps because her dreams last night had been so graphic. She'd woken once with the feel of his lips on hers, so real she'd had to touch her mouth with her fingers to be sure it hadn't happened.

"Bring a jacket. It'll be chilly by the time we have the fireworks," Kelly advised.

Chelsea went inside, clipped a fanny pack on and stuffed a jacket inside it. With a straw hat to protect her from the sun, she rejoined her friend and set off along the lakeside path.

Her mouth was dry by the time they covered the two or three hundred feet between her cabin and Pierce's home. The scent of sizzling meat and the sound of children's laughter filled the air. Volleyball, baseball and a game of horseshoes were in progress. Several people swam or rode in paddleboats about the lake.

And a good time was had by all, she thought, mocking her nervousness as she and Kelly approached the cooking area.

Pierce and his brother-in-law, Jim, manned the huge barbecue grill, where steaks, chicken, hot dogs and hamburgers cooked.

"Hey, about time," Jim called out. "We need help."

"What should we do?" Kelly asked, volunteering for duty. She grabbed an apron and tossed one to Chelsea.

Chelsea had no choice but to smile, don the apron and get to work. Jim assigned her to slicing tomatoes and onions while Kelly set out condiments and bags of chips.

Pierce had been laughing and talking when the women arrived. Now he was silent. Chelsea felt like an intruder.

"Hey, Doc," a male voice called. Holt Tanner separated himself from a crowd of friends and came over. "I heard you finished the autopsy yesterday."

Chelsea admitted she had.

"Will the report be ready tomorrow?" he asked.

Around Pierce's age, the lawman shared the same intense intelligence and curiosity that Pierce had displayed about the case yesterday.

"Yes. In fact, it's ready now. I printed it out this morning," she told him.

"Great. Let's go get—"

"You're off duty this evening," Pierce broke into the conversation. "The report can wait until tomorrow."

The quick warning glance he flashed Chelsea told her he didn't want the news about Harriet Martel to be disclosed today.

"Holt, how about meeting in my office at nine in the morning?" He flicked another glance her way. "Dr. Kearns, will you be available?"

"Yes."

"Good. We'll discuss it then."

"I'd better tell the sheriff," Holt said, peering around the lake. "He's interested in the case and would probably want to attend the meeting."

"I don't want anyone there but you and Chel— Dr. Kearns."

Deputy Tanner stared at the mayor for a moment, then shrugged. "Sure. I'll be there. See you, Doc."

Chelsea had met the lawman Monday afternoon when she arrived in Rumor. He'd told her of the arrangements for her work at the morgue and directed her to the lake house Kelly had put at her disposal. Chelsea had liked the deputy's no-nonsense direct-ness and his easy mannerisms.

After he ambled off, Pierce looked her way. "Is the cabin satisfactory? You have everything you need?"

"Yes, it's a lovely place. I'm quite happy there."

"Good. Call the office if something doesn't work. They'll send a man over."

She realized the cabin must belong to the resort, rather than to Kelly and Jim as she'd thought, and therefore to Pierce. He was her host for the duration of her vacation.

"Thank you," she said, and smiled graciously while her heart jumped in alarm. This could get complicated.

Pierce gave her a keen glance as if noting the lack of real warmth in her thanks, as if he knew she wouldn't have accepted accommodations there had she known it belonged to him. His gaze hardened.

Kelly gave him a poke in the ribs. "I hate to mention this, oh great chef, but the hot dogs are burning."

He moved the blackened ones to the back of the grill. "Ring the dinner bell, smart mouth," he ordered.

Chelsea smiled at the teasing between the two. Unlike her family, the Daltons were closely knit. Their father had died when Pierce was thirteen. He and Kelly had pitched in to help their mom make ends meet on her housekeeping earnings. Kelly and Pierce had made being poor sound like an adventure. Chelsea knew it must have been hard.

Her own family had been split by divorce when she was four. Each parent had remarried and had two other children, leaving her the odd man out in each family.

Poor, pitiful me, she mocked the odd sorrow she couldn't quite shake.

The ringing of the bell brought a flock of hungry kids and parents to the table where she and Kelly toiled for the next two and a half hours, keeping everyone supplied with napkins, paper plates, tons of chips, mustard, relish and mayo while the men served an equal amount of meat.

"Hey, the end of the line," Kelly sang out in relief. "We can fix a plate and sit down."

Chelsea had to admit she was happy for a respite, too. Holding a soda can in one hand and a full plate with the other, she glanced around the picnic area.

"Come on," Pierce told them. "There's a table on my deck where we can sit."

His house nestled in the trees that screened the resort from view. Like hers, it was made of stone on the bottom and logs on the top half with lots of windows to let in light. The deck wound around several trees near the edge of the creek. They settled in padded chairs at the patio table.

"Hi, Dr. Kelly," a little boy called out.

"Hi, Dr. Kelly," a girl around the same age echoed.

"Two of my favorite patients," Kelly said, waving at the pair. "They're twins and just full of mischief."

Chelsea noted the longing on Kelly's face as she watched the twin brother and sister run across the lawn and join a man and woman at a table by the lake. They looked like a happy family.

"Shall we tell them our surprise?" Kelly asked her husband.

"Sure."

"Jim and I think we're going to become parents in about eight months," Kelly said softly.

Chelsea's throat closed up at the exchange of gentle glances between husband and wife. Kelly was also thirty-four. It was time they were starting their family.

"Congratulations," she said, truly glad for them, but envious, too. They'd married right after Kelly got out of medical school. Her residency had been hard on the marriage, but they had gotten through the tough times. Now they radiated quiet happiness as they shared their news.

Pierce laughed. "Wait till Mom hears she's going to be a grandmother. She'll buy out the toy stores by Christmas."

"We're thinking of adding on another bedroom to the house," Jim said. "You think your construction crew could work us in?"

"Sure. You need to finish replacing the plumbing in that old barn, too. And the wiring. How about moving to one of the cabins and letting us do it all at one time? It'll save you money in the long run."

"Talk to your sister," Jim said.

"Sis?"

"You know I hate moving," Kelly wailed.

Chelsea knew the family had lost their home after their father had died. Finding places they could afford to rent had been touch-and-go during those early years until Pierce got out of high school and started working full-time.

He'd gotten his real estate license and started his own construction company by the time he was twenty-one. At twenty-five, he'd moved his mother into a brand-new home of her own, and she'd never had to move again.

When he'd bought the lake property, he'd built this marvelous home for himself two years ago. When Kelly had told her about it, Chelsea had thought he would be bringing a bride to his secluded retreat soon.

Why hadn't he ever married?

She stared into the distance as she contemplated the question. No answer came to her. After a bit she watched the scene by the lake while she finished the meal. Seeing the twins, she smiled as they organized a game of tag with several other kids, the brother and sister ironing out the rules between them, while the others waited for the final decision. Born leaders, they were.

Her eyes misted over. She wasn't getting any younger, but a family wasn't in the cards. Her gaze swung around like a magnet pointing to the lodestar.

Pierce was watching her, an unreadable expression in his eyes. For a moment, she couldn't look away. Then she did and hoped he hadn't detected the longing that filled her to the point she hurt someplace deep inside.

Life was what it was, she reminded herself. She hadn't time for adolescent yearning. She had a job to do—help the police find the person who would take the life of a woman and her child, then hide it as a suicide.

A local, she'd concluded. A stranger would have simply left the area. Only someone who lived there would need to cover his or her tracks. She wondered if Pierce had figured that out.

Chapter Two

Chelsea didn't want to be at his house, Pierce realized when she announced she should get back to the other cabin. She didn't want to be around him, period.

For some reason that made him angry. It also stirred up a demon that made him want to make sure she was as aware of his presence as he was of hers.

He cursed long and silently, but it did no good. All the old feelings she'd once evoked in him were on a rampage. He wanted to kiss her, to yell at her, to... to... Hell, he didn't know.

"You can't leave," Kelly insisted. "We have to stay for the fireworks."

"We'll have to move closer," Pierce said. "The trees screen us from the east side of the lake."

His sister had an answer for that. "Let's go over to Chelsea's place. It has a perfect view of the entire lake."

Before anyone could protest, Kelly was on her feet and leading the way. Pierce gritted his teeth. He knew his sister when she was in her full-speed-ahead mode.

"Another beer?" he asked Jim.

Jim cast him an amused but sympathetic glance. "Yes, thanks."

Pierce retrieved a couple of bottles from his fridge and followed the other three across the stepping stones in the creek to the other house that was basically a smaller version of his own. He didn't know what Kelly and Chelsea were planning, but he wanted no part of it.

Eight years ago she'd chosen a residency in forensic pathology at a prestigious university hospital back east over a future with him. Who could blame her?

For a moment he recalled how she'd looked— her eyes shining and filled with awe that she'd been accepted in the program. Then had come an expression of uncertainty, as if she didn't know what to do with him. He'd wished her well and made it clear he'd never been interested in a long-term relationship with her.

So what was she doing back in Montana? Knowing his sister, the answer wouldn't be good news for him.

Heaving a rough sigh, he carried the beers over to the deck bordering the lake and settled in a chair already in place for him...next to Chelsea.

"Good timing," Kelly said. "The fireworks are just starting."

Seeing Chelsea slap at her arm, he recalled that she seemed to attract every mosquito for a mile around and developed big lumps from their bites. "I'll get some bug spray," he told her.

"I have some." She went into the cabin and returned in a minute, smelling of citronella. She waved the spray can at them. "Anyone else?"

Kelly held out a hand. "Yes. Honey, I'll spray your back, then would you do mine?" she said to Jim.

Pierce observed while the couple took care of each other. When he glanced at Chelsea, she, too, was watching, a quietness about her that was unsettling.

Huh. She'd chosen her career over all else. If she regretted it, that was just too bad.

Pleased that he was able to maintain the right psychological distance from her, he relaxed, took a swig of beer and enjoyed the first burst of fireworks over the lake.

Chelsea woke fully alert and ready to get on with the day. She had three hours before the nine o'clock meeting in Pierce's office. Plenty of time for a swim and workout.

She donned a bathing suit and headed out the back door to the deck. The lake wasn't deep enough to dive in at this point, but she could wade out to waist deep, then swim some laps. She set her waterproof watch for twenty minutes.

The air was already comfortably warm, an indication that the day would be another scorcher. What had happened to those cool Montana nights?

She waded into the lake, then laughed as chills raced along her thighs. The water hadn't warmed up. She plunged in up to her neck, sighted a cottonwood as a marker and swam steadily up and down the shore between the deck and the tree for twenty minutes.

Finished, she raced for the deck and the towel she'd left behind. "Oh," she said softly upon seeing Pierce standing there in snug jeans and a long-sleeved shirt, a steaming mug of coffee in his hand.

He tossed her the towel, his gaze colder than the icy water of the lake.

"Good morning," she said, determined to be cheerful around him. It was time to get over the past and move on.

"That is the skimpiest bathing suit I've ever seen," he told her.

She looked at her two-piece suit. It was cut high on the legs as all of them were, but it wasn't a string bikini or anything like that. "Surely not," she said airily.

Uh-oh, wrong thing to say. He looked as if he would like to choke her.

"That outfit might be modest for the city, but around here, folks dress more circumspectly."

She couldn't help it. She burst out laughing.

Pierce glared at her.

She laughed harder. "I'm sorry," she finally managed to say, not at all sincerely. "It's just that you sound so pompous and indignant, not at all like the Pierce who dared me to go skinny-dipping in the pool at my apartment building at three o'clock on a January morning."

He looked rather taken aback that she would bring up the passionate past, but she'd realized last night that they couldn't pretend it didn't exist.

"I'm not here to discuss the past," he informed her. "I have other things to do than watch out for you."

"No one asked you to look after me."

Gesturing toward her outfit, now hidden by the towel, he stalked toward her. "If some of the guys working here see you like that, they'll take it as an open invitation to visit. I won't have them distracted by a siren from the city."

Chelsea rubbed the end of the towel over her dripping hair. She'd never been called a siren before.

"If it's for my benefit," he continued, "you're wasting your time. I have more important things to do than get mixed up with you again."

Astounded at this proclamation, she stared at him. The situation was no longer amusing. Anger flamed. "Pompous *and* egotistical," she murmured loud enough for him to hear. "You have changed in eight years."

His gaze drifted all the way down to her feet and back to her face. "You're on my turf now. Watch yourself."

With that sage advice, he strode off, heading back to his house in a manner that suggested a charging bull. She leaned against the railing and frowned at his back, her temper unappeased.

"You'd better watch yourself, too," she called to him. "City sirens are hard to resist."

His shoulders stiffened, but he stalked on.

Feeling that she'd gotten the last word in, she shivered and hurried inside to a warm shower. The day was off to a good start. She could hardly wait to see how the rest of it went.

"I don't believe it. Miss Martel?" Holt Tanner said when Chelsea related her findings.

"Nevertheless, it's true."

"Four months," he repeated. "Who was the father?"

"He didn't leave a calling card."

Pierce shot a warning glance at her flippant remark. He still wasn't very happy with her. Fine. She could live with that. In fact, it made things easier. There would be no more dreams of hot kisses and roaming hands—

"And you can definitely rule out suicide?"

She nodded to the lawman.

Holt paced to the window. "I don't want the news of a pregnancy to get out. It's the only thing we know that the killer also knows. Maybe he'll slip up sooner or later."

Chelsea was pleased that the deputy was on the same mental track with her. "He's local."

"Yeah, I realized that as soon as you said she was pregnant. Do you think she was blackmailing him—demanding money for her silence?" The lawman stared into the middle distance, deep in thought.

"Or demanding marriage," Pierce suggested. He rubbed a hand over his face. "What else don't we know about the mysterious Miss Martel, gruff and reclusive librarian that she was?"

Holt turned a chair around and straddled it, his forearms crossed over the back. "I've been checking her records and accounts. By Rumor standards, she was rich."

"Harriet Martel?" Pierce was obviously startled at this new disclosure.

Holt nodded. "She'd been investing her money for years. There's a sizable inheritance."

"Who gets it?"

"I don't know if there's a will. The only relatives are her sister, Louise Holmes, and Louise's son, Colby. Gossip has it that Colby is denying his aunt would have killed herself." Holt frowned. "The thought of murder makes people nervous."

"It could scare off the tourists, too. The city council is planning another event after the success of the Crazy Moon Festival last month. It'll be a bust if no one shows up for it."

Chelsea listened quietly as the men discussed the case and the consequences for the small town that depended on tourist dollars for cash flow. Murder spread a wide ripple across a narrow pond in a community such as Rumor.

Holt snapped his fingers. "In a murder case in one town, they tested every male's DNA. We could do that."

Chelsea grimaced. "The perp paid another man to take the test for him, so the results didn't do any good."

"Not until the man's conscience finally got the better of him and he confessed. The perp was then tested and found to be guilty," Holt reminded her.

Pierce dismissed the idea. "The court would have to agree it was necessary, too, else it's an invasion of privacy. I don't think a judge in the county would condone widespread testing."

The men were silent as they sought another avenue to pinpoint the murderer.

"Chelsea, can you help out?" Pierce asked.

"Of course. What do you have in mind?"

"Holt, do you mind if Chelsea looks over all the evidence? I can vouch for her discretion," he added when the lawman shot her a troubled glance. "You can take her out to Harriet's house and let her poke around. Maybe she'll find an angle we've overlooked." He smiled grimly. "Harriet was murdered on Saturday night, during the last weekend of the festival. Six days ago. We need this case wrapped up."

Holt stood. "Are you available now? I'm free this morning, but I have to present evidence at a hearing this afternoon."

"Yes," she said.

Pierce rose when she did. He glanced at his watch. "I have a council meeting shortly. Chelsea, can you join me for lunch at twelve sharp?"

Confused by the invitation, which sounded more like a command, she agreed to meet him. "Here?"

"At my place. I want to discuss your findings in private." He turned to the deputy. "Have you turned in Chelsea's report to the sheriff?"

"Not yet. I'll be seeing him at five."

"Tell him I'll be at home this evening if he wants to come out and discuss it. I'd rather not say anything on the phone, especially a cell phone."

The hair crept up on Chelsea's neck at Pierce's ominous tone. Noting his deep frown as she and Holt left his office, she realized he was worried about the town and its citizens. As mayor, he had to be. There was a killer loose in their midst, and right now, only the three of them knew it, plus one other....

Ten minutes later, the lawman muttered an expletive when he turned into a narrow drive on a quiet side street. Another vehicle was parked next to the white cottage with its dark green shutters and colorful flower boxes and yellow crime-scene tape stretched across the front porch.

"Who is it?" she asked.

"The nephew. Colby Holmes. I'll wring his neck if he's touched anything."

The door was unlocked, eliciting another curse. Chelsea followed Holt inside. "Colby," he yelled.

"In here," a male voice called out.

Chelsea entered a room that was more an alcove than a full-size room, Holt on her heels. Bay windows let in the morning sunlight. Bookshelves lined every available wall, and a desk occupied the rest of the space.

A young man in his mid- to late-twenties sat on the floor in front of a bookcase. With brown eyes and hair and a restlessness that spoke of contained energy, the former rodeo star was attractive and determined as he returned the deputy's glare.

"What the hell are you doing, crossing a police line and messing around in here?" Holt demanded.

"Looking," came the reply.

"For what?"

"Proof that Aunt Harriet didn't commit suicide."

"Who said she did?"

The nephew narrowed his eyes at the deputy. "That's the rumor flying around town. It's a lie. My aunt may have been a recluse, but she wasn't a wimp who couldn't face life."

"So what's your theory?" the deputy challenged.

"She was murdered." The younger man finished flipping through the book, put it on the shelf and stood. His eyes cut to Chelsea. "Who's she?"

"Dr. Kearns. The medical examiner sent down from Billings."

"Mom said the cops had ordered an autopsy. Have you done it yet?"

"Yes."

"Well?" he said impatiently.

Chelsea held her temper with an effort. The men she'd met thus far in Rumor were an autocratic bunch. When she'd arrived Monday evening after working in Billings all day, the deputy had wanted her to start that night.

She'd refused. However, she'd spent all day Tuesday and most of Wednesday in the morgue. She'd checked and rechecked the evidence, which was in short supply. She'd promptly written up her report. Did that satisfy them? No way.

First the mayor, then the deputy had demanded firsthand information on the case. Now a third male was demanding to know her findings. She was tired of demands.

"Check with the sheriff," she advised.

"No information is going out until we finish investigating the case," Holt told the younger man. "If you've destroyed any evidence, I'll have your hide in jail so fast it'll make you dizzy. Stay out of it, Colby."

"Then find out the truth." He strode toward the door. "My aunt didn't commit suicide."

Chelsea and the lawman watched the nephew leave, then they turned back to the crime scene. "Where was her body found?" Chelsea asked.

For the next two hours they went over the cottage for any missed evidence. Chelsea noted the librarian had few personal effects in the neat little house. Other than a couple of pictures of Colby, plus one of his mother and the deceased woman, there was an absence of knickknacks.

However, there were plenty of books. Naturally. A librarian would have a passion for books. And for the man who'd killed her and the unborn child?

"Was the child his?" she murmured aloud. "Or had she gone to someone else, and that's what made him so furious?"

"Good question." Holt wiped the sweat from his brow. He looked tired and irritated. The temperature was in the nineties as predicted. He continued his inspection of the chair where Harriet Martel had died. It had already been combed for fibers and hairs.

On the table next to the chair was a novel. Chelsea read the title: *Dangerous Liaisons*. A bookmark near the end indicated the woman had been reading it prior to the murder.

An apt selection. The librarian's liaison had proved very dangerous.

Chelsea reached for the book, then stopped. She wasn't wearing latex gloves, so she was hesitant to touch anything. "Has everything been dusted for prints?"

Holt was now on his haunches studying the carpet. "Yeah. We didn't find many, and what few we did find belonged to Harriet or her family. A few others were too smudged to reveal anything. The whole place was wiped down before the perp left."

"Did you check the drains for hair? Are there any toothbrushes that are different?"

"We did all that."

Chelsea stepped nearer the chair. A sense of intense cold caused her to shiver.

The times when she was requested to attend a murder scene bothered her for days afterward. Maybe it was imagination, but she seemed to feel the anger and the agony, the tragic death scene that had resulted from uncontrolled emotion. A psychic she'd once met on a case had assured her it was real, that the energy caused by strife and grief lingered long after the deed.

Chelsea felt it now—the hot fury, then the cold, calculating anger, the sudden fear of the woman, the need to protect the child—

"It was for the child," she said. "Whatever started the conflict, it was for the child. The victim wanted to protect her baby."

"From what?" Holt asked, giving her a curious look.

"Scandal, perhaps. Or maybe he wanted her to get rid of it and she refused."

As soon as Chelsea said the words, she knew they were true. The cold in the room drove right down to her soul. It lingered near the chair where the librarian had died, like a ghost hovering there, silently imploring them to discover the truth and thus find her killer.

She stared at the worn chair. For a wealthy person the woman had lived very simply. The chair, table and lamp indicated this was her favorite reading spot.

A small stain marred the upholstery, but that was the only evidence of the violence that had taken place. Since the bullet hadn't exited, there was little bleeding and no splatter on the walls and floor.

A very neat murder with a small-caliber weapon such as a woman might have in the house to protect herself from intruders. The man would have known about the gun. Maybe he gave it to her.

"You ready to go?" the deputy asked.

Wrapping her arms across her chest, she nodded. "Yes, I'm ready."

The return trip was short. The deputy parked on Main Street in front of the sheriff's office. After he went inside, she realized she had a half hour before she met with Pierce. Seeing a diner up the street, she went there and ordered a cup of coffee.

A newspaper had been left on a chair at the table. She picked it up and read the headline: Suicide in Rumor.

The story recounted Harriet Martel's life in the town and how she'd transformed the library into a quiet oasis of learning. She'd instituted several story hours for different age groups and arranged for tutoring sessions between volunteers and students who needed help.

All in all she appeared to have been a good person, apparently dedicated to her job. Who had made her forget her basic values? Who was the man she had so foolishly loved?

Colby Holmes slid into the chair opposite her. "I want to talk to you," he said.

"Mr. Holmes, you have my sympathy about your aunt, but the work I do in a case like this is strictly confidential. You'll have to ask the sheriff—"

"In a case like what?" he interrupted.

She gazed at him without answering.

"If it was suicide, why all the secrecy? Coffee," he practically snarled at the teenage waitress, who scurried off in the face of his anger. He turned back to Chelsea. "Why an autopsy in the first place? Why call in the state's top forensic expert to perform it?"

She took a drink and watched him warily over the rim of the thick white cup.

The waitress plunked a mug and a cream pitcher on the table and departed.

"Murder, that's why," he answered the questions he raised. "What have you found out? I know you know more than you're telling. She was my relative. I have a right—"

"What's going on here?" Pierce asked in a low tone. He stopped by the table and leaned over Colby. "Holt Tanner says you're interfering in the investigation and possibly tampering with the crime scene. That could earn you several years in the pen."

Colby gave the mayor a sarcastic grin. "I didn't tamper with any evidence. I was looking for some. Holt must have missed something."

"Why do you say that?"

Colby tapped the newspaper headline. "Because Aunt Harriet was too strong-minded to do something like that. I wasn't around my aunt a lot, but she was a forceful woman. Look how she straightened this town out on how to run the library. When she said jump, the city council did."

Pierce studied the younger man for a long twenty seconds. Chelsea stilled herself for a confrontation. Pierce surprised her when he placed a hand on Colby's shoulder.

"I agree. She was one determined woman, practical and fair-minded. Suicide seemed out of character to me, too. I asked for Dr. Kearns to do the autopsy and lend the sheriff's department a hand because she is the best. Let the law do its job, okay?"

The two men eyed each other, one angry and suspicious, the other calm and certain.

At last Colby nodded. "I'd like to know what you turn up," he requested.

"I'll see that you get a full report," Pierce promised.

After Colby left, Pierce tilted his head toward the street. "Ready to go? I have to get back for a meeting at two this afternoon." He sighed and added, "I hate meetings."

Instead of riding with him, she drove her own car to her cabin, then walked the short distance to his. She'd wondered what he was going to serve, then discovered he'd bought two lunches at the diner. That's what had brought him in while she was being grilled by the nephew.

"Barbecued chicken, your favorite," he said, setting the containers on the patio table. He'd also provided two large cups of iced tea, hers with lemon.

Taking a chair, she joined him in the meal, her mind going like a buzz saw. Pierce had asked for her help with the case. She hadn't known that. He'd remembered that she took lemon in her tea.

Not that these tidbits meant anything, she reminded her suddenly buoyant spirits. She sighed quietly. Whatever they had shared was now long gone, but it had been a lovely time out of time while it lasted.

As soon as they finished eating, he asked, "Did you see anything interesting at Harriet's house?"

Chelsea brought her wayward thoughts in line. "She was a neat person. Her house wasn't cluttered. She liked flowers and she was fond of her sister and nephew. There were no signs of a past of any kind. Where did she go to college? Where was she born? What was she hiding?"

"I don't think she was hiding anything. Her diplomas are in her office at the library. She has several. She earned a PhD after she moved here, but she didn't like being called Dr. Martel."

"It's obvious she was very intelligent," Chelsea said.

Pierce studied her, a questioning frown on his face. "But you see a contradiction in her actions?"

"Yes. How does a smart, independent and wealthy woman get mixed up with someone who would shoot her and try to make it look like suicide?"

"You're the expert. You tell me."

Chelsea hesitated, then said, "He was very controlling. I think he wanted her to get rid of the baby. She refused. That triggered the quarrel."

Pierce leaned toward her, excitement flashing through his eyes. "Can you profile him for us?"

"I can give you some ideas on his personality." She considered the evidence she'd seen and been given by the lawman. "He's used to command, and he hates to be thwarted. He has a temper, which he's generally learned to control."

"But not always," Pierce muttered.

"No, not always. He's in his forties, maybe early fifties. Miss Martel was forty-three. At any rate, he was mature enough to control the first wave of panic and think through corrective steps. He wiped down his fingerprints, then set up the suicide. He was smart enough to use her gun."

"There's no record she had one," Pierce said.

Chelsea shrugged. "The slug was a twenty-two, a caliber a woman would be comfortable with—not too big, but powerful enough for close range, say if a burglar was in the house. He probably gave her the gun and insisted she keep it."

Pierce was silent for a long minute. "Anything else?"

"He would be drawn to positions of power. If in the army, he'd be an officer. In civilian life, he could be a cop or a CEO. If he owned a company, he'd be a tyrant. To attract a woman like Harriet Martel, he'd have to be intelligent. He'd also be charming. Both are good skills for public office. He'd more likely hold an elective office rather than an appointed one."

"Why?"

"Self-preservation. Other men would be afraid of him. He's ambitious and ruthless. Utterly ruthless."

"A person would have to be without conscience to kill his lover and his child. Is that your conclusion?"

"Yes."

Pierce grimaced. "I wish I knew what to think. I can't conceive of a murderer walking around loose in *my* town. I know everybody within ten miles of the city limits and probably half the rest of the county, too. You and Holt say the man is local. I find that hard to believe."

Anger blazed from his eyes as he glared at her. She went on the defensive. "Believe what you wish. Perhaps you'd like to bring someone else in on the case. I can give you a name. I trained under one of the FBI's foremost forensic investigators my last year of school."

"So Kelly said." He waved a hand in dismissal of her suggestion. "You're the best, or else I wouldn't have asked for you."

Her eyes met his and locked. For an eternity they gazed at each other, questions and awareness rushing in rivers of unappeased hunger between them.

"Damnation," he muttered.

Then he reached for her.

Chapter Three

Chelsea knew she should tell him no. She ordered her lips to form the word. But she didn't utter it. This moment was too much like her dreams the past few nights.

Then his mouth met hers and all the wonder and desire of the past rolled over her. She knew he felt it, too. A shudder went through him as he held her closer, and she was instantly aware of the hardness of his body and of his hunger.

She arched her back and pressed against him, eager for completion that had been missing for eight years. Tears burned the back of her eyes as she realized just how much she'd missed this…missed him….

His hands, warm and supple, roamed her back, her hips, along her thighs, up her sides, then paused for an instant before sliding upward once more. He turned slightly so he could cup her breast in one hand while the other slid to her hip to caress in a kneading motion.

"Too long," he muttered, releasing her mouth and skipping kisses along her jaw and down her throat. "It's been too long."

"Yes." She touched his face, combed her fingers through the thick strands of his hair, loving the feel, the texture of him against her palms. "I've missed—"

She stopped the words, not wanting to admit there'd been few dates and no serious relationship in her life since they'd parted.

"This," he finished for her. "I know. I told myself I wouldn't want you again."

"Then don't. Let me go."

Anger joined the flames of passion in his eyes. "I can't. It's too strong. You have a hold over me...."

He shook his head. She understood the frustration, the longing that wouldn't let up, the failure of logic and all the reasons they shouldn't be doing this.

When he lifted her to the railing and pushed between her thighs, fitting their bodies intimately into place, her bones became as pliant as taffy. When he moved against her, her mind went cloudy.

They kissed endlessly, a wildness running through her blood and echoing in the beat of his heart against her breasts. Fighting the tidal wave of hunger was useless. She clung to him, wanting the hot bliss that only he stirred to life in her.

"Why?" he said at one point, his eyes licking over her in restless flames of need. "Why does it have to be you?"

Hurt, she tried to draw away, but he wouldn't let her. She turned her face from his rampaging mouth. He caught her head between his hands and held her face so he could gaze into her eyes.

"It's always been this way for us, hasn't it?" he demanded huskily. "Wild and necessary. Primitive and unexplained. The call of blood to blood."

She shook her head, unable to summon words in her defense but feeling that she should.

"Irresistible," he whispered.

He took her mouth again, fanning the passion that flowed like lava between them, burning all sense and good intentions to a crisp, leaving only the hunger, the terrible, terrible hunger. She moaned as he caressed her breasts, his thumbs brushing over the sensitive tips so that they contracted into hard points of ecstasy.

"I have to see you, all of you," he told her. "It's like being starved, then coming upon a feast. I have to have it all."

"Yes," she said, knowing exactly what he meant. "Yes."

With fingers that trembled ever so little, he unfastened her blouse and pulled it from her slacks. Eyes narrowed impatiently, he checked her bra, then slid his hands around her and unfastened the hooks.

Slowly, torturously, he pushed the satin upward, out of the way. Then he simply looked, his lashes lowered sexily over the flaming passion she saw in his gaze.

"Beautiful," he said, and kissed the yearning tips, then feathered his tongue over each one.

She clutched his shoulders as the world spun out of control. When he lifted her breasts and paid special attention to them with his lips and his hands, she couldn't keep from crying out as the wonder of his touch filled her.

He lifted her from the railing and set her on her feet. Taking her hand, he said, "Let's go."

In the cabin, its air cool compared to the heat of the deck, she tried to think, but her mind refused to cooperate. She realized she didn't want caution and reason and all the things she'd practiced all her life.

Going into the bedroom with him, she stopped when he did and faced him, her heart rushing its beat at the intensity in his gaze.

"I have protection at my place," he said softly, his eyes locked with hers. "Would you feel better if we used it?"

She blinked in uncertainty. "I can't conceive," she finally said. "I had polyps removed, but there's scar tissue."

He laid a finger over her lips, then lingered to caress her gently. "Kelly told me. I'm safe, but I wanted to make sure you were comfortable."

Chelsea looked away from his probing gaze, touched by his consideration in ways she didn't want to admit. He'd always had the ability to reach inside and touch the lonely places she tried to hide.

He tipped her chin up. "Chelsea?"

"Yes," she whispered. "I'm comfortable."

He heaved a breath as if he'd been unsure of her answer. "I'm not. I'm burning up."

With a grin that caused her heart to flip, he pushed the shirt and bra off her shoulders until they fell to the floor. His eyes darkened as he stared at her.

Her breasts were flushed, the tips a dusky pink. Passion's bloom, he had once called the telltale rosy hue her body took on when he caressed her intimately. She'd been embarrassed at the obvious signs of passion when they'd first become lovers.

The smart of tears surprised her as she remembered how sweetly reassuring he'd been, how he'd encouraged her to show the need, to tell him what she wanted. It had been a thrilling time of mutual exploration and discovery of the passionate side of nature.

He quickly stripped his shirt off and moved closer until he could brush her nipples, teasing her with slow dry strokes of wiry hairs across her as he had earlier with the wet caresses of his tongue.

She closed her eyes and tilted her head until she could feel the brush of her hair along her back. Holding on to his powerful shoulders, she let inhibitions go and gloried in the tactile sensations of touch.

When her knees went weak, she swayed against him, her body curving into his as naturally as a willow bending before the wind.

"Wait," Pierce said huskily. He shucked his clothing, then helped her get out the rest of her things. They fell onto the bed as one.

Then there was skin against skin as their arms and legs entwined naturally, in ways never forgotten.

He knew there was danger in her embrace, but it didn't matter—not now. If there was a price to pay for this moment, he'd worry about it tomorrow.

"So sweet," he murmured, taking her lips in a thousand kisses that fed a part of him he didn't know was starving. "And so dangerous."

"Yes," she agreed, "but so good. I've never forgotten how good it was."

Stroking intimately, he found she was ready. So was he. He rolled over her lithe form, settling between her thighs as she opened to him, her eyes on his face, shining with trust as well as need.

It gave him pause, then he whispered, "Take me in you."

As if it had been hours rather than years, he merged his body with hers. As she shifted to accommodate him, he realized she was experiencing some discomfort.

Puzzled, he stopped. "Am I hurting you?"

She shook her head. "It's okay."

Which didn't tell him a thing. "It's been a long

time for you, hasn't it?" he asked, feeling his way through the moment.

She closed her eyes. "Yes. Don't talk."

When she wrapped herself around him and urged him deeper, he couldn't hold back. He sank into the smooth hot depths, a shudder rippling over him as he held back the too-ready climax. He wanted hours with her…hours…

Chelsea gasped when he carefully started moving, bringing her back to passionate intensity with his lips and his hands. Flames danced through her as she touched him in all the places he liked. She savored hearing his breath catch and his heart pound when she grew bold with her caresses.

He laid his head on the pillow beside hers. "Wait," he whispered. "We're going too fast."

"I want you…*now*."

Catching her hands, he kissed the tip of her nose, a funny smile on his mouth. It was almost sad.

"You were always impatient," he scolded good-naturedly. He tousled her hair. "A little red-headed, green-eyed ginger cat who wanted it all right away."

"You wanted it to last," she said, remembering their ardent love play, rich with the nuances that flowed between lovers.

His low laughter filtered through her like dappled sunlight on water, warm and sparkling. "We can have both," he murmured, then proceeded to show her.

With sure touches that spoke of their experiences

long ago, he brought her to pleasure so intense she cried out in shocked delight. He smothered her cries with kisses and his own panting efforts at control. When at last she lay still beneath him, he turned them to the side and smoothed the damp clinging tendrils from her face.

With her nose snuggled against his chest, she floated in some peaceful sphere where nothing touched her—not doubts or worries or anything of a mundane nature.

She murmured contentedly when he began moving again. It had always amazed her how quickly she could respond again when she was in his arms.

"I want you again," she told him in wonder. "How can I want you again so soon?"

"Because," Pierce said, and rolled over her, finding the sweet nest between her thighs. "I won't be able to stop this time," he warned as the banked passion flared with astounding speed.

She opened her eyes, dark green now with passion. "I don't want you to stop."

He breathed deeply when she moved against him, away, then arched up to meet his downward thrust. His mind glazed over as the hunger took hold.

At her whimpering gasp of need, he thrust deeper. He guided her hand between them, encouraging her to ride the tide between them while he plunged into the hot center of her, nearly going over the edge but managing to hold it together until she cried out as the pleasure overcame all other senses. He thrust once more and went into the mindless abyss with her.

It was a long time before either of them moved.

The tick of the clock finally penetrated the haven where he drifted in perfect peace. The ringing of the telephone jarred the tranquility of the afternoon. He reached past her shoulder, picked up the receiver and held it to her ear.

"Uh, Chelsea, this is Kelly."

Chelsea stiffened as reality forcefully returned. "Hi, Kelly," she said, using her friend's name to warn Pierce to be silent.

"Fran is looking for Pierce," Kelly said. "She's his secretary. She says he had a meeting at two. She called me when he didn't show up or answer his phone or beeper."

Chelsea was intensely aware that his head was pressed to hers so he could hear the conversation. She looked a question at him. He shook his head.

"Should I go over to his house and see if he's there?" Chelsea asked.

Kelly didn't reply for a heartbeat. "Uh, no. I was hoping he was at your place." She laughed. "Actually, I thought you two might be…uh, how should I put this—in the sack? The sparks were flying from more than the fireworks last night."

The blood rushed to Chelsea's head so fast she went dizzy. "Don't get any ideas," she advised her friend, and carefully kept her gaze from Pierce. "I'll tell him you're looking for him. If I see him."

"Okay, thanks. By the way, I'm having a birthday dinner for Mom Saturday night. That's tomorrow. You're to come."

They said goodbye and hung up. When she glanced at Pierce, he seemed deep in thought. She squirmed to remind him he was nearly lying on her.

Muttering a curse, he sat up. "I'm supposed to be at a meeting." He flung on clothing as fast he could.

She pushed upright. With a pillow behind her back and the sheet covering her, she watched him silently, no expression in her eyes. She didn't know if she felt regret, anger or what. She wondered about him, but not for long.

"Stupid," he said aloud. He thrust his feet into his shoes. "That was stupid. I thought I was immune to you. What a laugh."

She blinked back the raw hurt, but said nothing. His disgust was directed at himself and his weakness—stupidity, to use his term—in succumbing to passion. Darkness gathered inside her, a void that carried the weight of the world in it. Ah, well, she hadn't expected a rose garden....

"I thought it wouldn't matter, who you were or that we'd once been lovers. It doesn't matter. I'll be the one to walk away this time."

Her eyes widened at the implied accusation. "You did last time."

"Like hell."

She reviewed her memories. "You did. You said you didn't want a long-term relationship."

He strode toward the door. "I still don't." Then he walked out.

She stayed in bed until she heard his car start, then leave, the purr of the engine rapidly dwindling on the still afternoon air. Only then did she shower and dress in fresh clothing and go out on the deck to read.

Instead of opening her book, she sat there, staring at the mountain peaks to the west. Once she'd thought Pierce was her knight in shining armor and they would live in a beautiful castle in an enchanted kingdom.

She smiled in sympathy for her younger, more idealistic self. In truth, she'd never expected a fairy-tale ending, but she'd thought they would marry and have children and grow old together.

Now, eight years later, she was wiser and more skeptical about life and love and happily ever after. But it had been a lovely illusion.

Chelsea woke from a light doze when a car door slammed. "Around back," she called out. She expected Kelly to appear, but two men came around the corner. One was Holt Tanner. The other was a man she hadn't met, but she recognized him as the sheriff.

"Dr. Kearns, Sheriff Reingard," Holt introduced them.

She stood and held out her hand. "Please, call me Chelsea, both of you."

The sheriff took her hand and held it. "I'm Dave. It's good to have you onboard, Chelsea. I was against bringing in outsiders, but Pierce convinced me we needed the best in this case. From the details in your report, I think he was right. Welcome to our community."

Chelsea sized him up. Early fifties. Dark eyes. Surprising, given that his hair was blond. He was graying at the temples, she noted, and his face was somewhat florid. A couple of inches under six feet. His grip was firm, his hand smooth. Not overweight but at the top of his range. Nothing a good exercise program wouldn't fix.

She eased her hand from his and thanked him. "Can I get you something to drink? Tea? Coffee? Soda?"

"A soda," the sheriff requested.

"Tea, if you have it," Holt said.

She prepared iced tea for her and the deputy, a soft drink for the sheriff. After she returned to the deck, they went over her report. The sheriff questioned her extensively on the results of the autopsy.

"Four months," the lawman murmured, gazing out over the lake. "Harriet Martel." He shook his head in disbelief.

"Pierce said he'd never seen her with anyone," Chelsea mentioned. "Did you?"

The sheriff laughed, a deep, pleasant sound. "I'm not out on the town very much myself. My wife and I have five children. I spend my spare time at the soccer and baseball fields in summer. In the winter we rescue hunters from blizzards." He shook his head in exasperation, then laughed again.

Chelsea smiled, too, amused as the sheriff reached into a pocket and removed a pistachio. He ate it absently and tossed the shell over the railing into the lake, obviously lost in thought. She wondered if she should make a citizen's arrest for littering or maybe polluting the lake.

"Well," he said at last, "here's what I think we should do. Holt, take Chelsea over to the library this afternoon and question the staff. Maybe she can pick up on something we missed, sort of a woman-to-woman thing, especially with Molly Brewster. Molly found Harriet," he explained to Chelsea.

"She went to Harriet's house, thinking she must be sick or hurt when she didn't show up for work," Holt added. He glanced at his watch. "It's nearly four. We'd better go. The library closes soon."

"Uh, I guess I don't need to remind you not to give out any information," the sheriff told her.

Chelsea observed the sheriff, knowing he wasn't going to like her next words. "People will figure out something is going on if the investigation continues."

A frown appeared on the still-attractive features of the lawman as he thought the situation through. He ate another pistachio. "I understand Colby Holmes is spreading the word that his aunt was murdered," he finally said. "I suppose we can admit that much, but don't mention the pregnancy. As Holt said, that's our ace in the hole."

"Right." Chelsea insisted on driving herself into town when Holt offered her a ride. She had to stop by the grocery on the way back and pick up something for dinner, she explained. Although nothing appealed to her, she mused as she followed the lawmen along Main Street.

She parked at the library and waited while Holt dropped the sheriff off at the office, then parked his patrol car, an SUV with a rack of lights on top, beside hers. They went inside as a young woman came to the door, key in hand.

"I'm sorry," the woman said. "We're just closing."

Holt nodded. "Go ahead. We're here to talk to you."

Molly Brewster was twenty-seven, of average height with wavy blond hair and blue eyes. Chelsea recalled that she was from Wyoming and worked as an assistant librarian. She'd been hired by Harriet Martel eighteen months ago.

Rage could make a person much stronger than usual, but Chelsea, studying the slender librarian, didn't think Molly could have sustained fury long enough to accomplish all that needed doing at the crime scene, assuming she had a motive to kill her boss in the first place.

Holt introduced the women, then stepped back, leaving the questioning up to Chelsea.

She started out with general information, recapping what she already knew. The other library workers were adult volunteers or teenagers from the high school who got credit for their help. She asked about each of them and their hours of work.

She also noted Molly was nervous and apprehensive. The woman kept looking toward the front door, then a side entrance as they talked.

Chelsea decided to go straight to the point. "Who might have had a reason to dislike Miss Martel?"

Molly gasped and clutched her chest. She was slow in answering. "No one. I mean, Miss Martel was strict and all, but she wasn't mean or anything like that. She did a lot for this town."

Hmm, admiration, not envy, in the tone, Chelsea decided, but why the gasp and the clutching of the chest?

"Was Miss Martel murdered?" Molly asked, her eyes big and frightened, as if she thought a serial killer was loose in the area and she was the next victim.

Chelsea shrugged. "We have to cover all the angles," she said as if this explained everything.

Holt cleared his throat behind her. She cast him a glance to let him know she wasn't going to give anything away, then turned back to Molly. "Who were her friends?"

"Well, she didn't have any." Molly seemed to realize the stark quality of the statement. "I mean...well, I was her friend, and the volunteers, of course."

"Of course," Chelsea murmured.

"But I never saw her with anyone. I mean, she didn't go out to dinner with friends or anything like that. She did have someone, though."

Chelsea waited, her heart upping its beat.

"I heard her talking to someone on the phone sometimes. Once I heard her mention a time…as if they planned to meet later that evening."

"Any idea who it was? Male? Female? Relative?"

Molly shook her head. "She never said, and I would never ask. Miss Martel didn't approve of people prying into other people's business."

Chelsea had already deduced the head librarian was a reclusive woman with a very secret life.

After several more questions about the victim's life and habits, Chelsea indicated she was finished.

Holt stepped forward. "Please keep the details of this discussion to yourself, Miss Brewster. This is an ongoing police investigation."

"Because she was murdered?" Molly asked again. "Her nephew says it was murder. He's told everyone in town."

Holt's jaw tightened. Chelsea thought he might have cracked a few teeth as he held in angry words until they were outside before muttering, "I'll strangle Colby with my bare hands."

"People were already speculating about the case," she said to soothe him and because she was sympathetic to the nephew, who, unfortunately, was correct.

"They would always wonder, even if we did conclude it was suicide."

"Huh," was his disgruntled reply.

"Well, I need to go to the grocery—"

"Hey, Chelsea," Kelly called out, stopping her car in the middle of Main Street. "Join me for dinner. Jim works late on Friday nights. I hate to eat alone."

This was a much better prospect than munching on a salad and sandwich from the grocery deli. "Okay."

"Meet me at the Calico Diner." Kelly waved and drove off, then turned the corner to circle back to the diner.

The driver of the car behind her waved, too. A local, Chelsea surmised, returning the greeting. An outsider would have sat on the horn instead of thoughtfully waiting while the conversation was concluded. Small towns could be nice.

"See you later," Holt said and climbed in the SUV, his lean face still set and angry.

Chelsea left her car in the library parking lot and walked to the diner. Inside, she looked for her friend. A waitress—second trimester pregnant, Chelsea automatically noted—motioned toward a table. Kelly was already there.

"The town is abuzz," Kelly confided when Chelsea slid into the chair opposite her.

"What about?"

"The murder of Harriet Martel, for one." Kelly grinned, which was certainly at odds with her news.

"And the fact that my brother's car was at your place during lunch and afterward…when he was supposed to be with the president of the Chamber of Commerce."

Chelsea groaned. Small towns were hotbeds of gossip, she revised her earlier assessment. She should remember that.

"Well?" Kelly demanded.

"We were discussing the Martel case."

"Was it murder?"

"I'm afraid so."

"How terrible," Kelly said in a near whisper, her sparkle dimmed by the news. "Who could have done it?"

At that moment the diner door swung open. The sheriff walked in and went to the counter. Pierce was right behind him.

He spotted them and came over, his face grim. "Who the hell did you tell about the murder?"

Chapter Four

"Really, Pierce," Kelly scolded. "Is that any way to greet a person?"

He pulled out a chair and sat down, his eyes on Chelsea. "Well?"

Chelsea debated between defending herself and telling him where to get off. "Ask the sheriff," she said coolly.

"It's all over town," Kelly said impatiently. "Colby has been broadcasting far and wide that his aunt didn't commit suicide."

Chelsea nodded. "People should be told the truth. You can't keep murder a secret."

"The sheriff said we were to keep a lid on it."

His manner was a direct challenge. Chelsea responded to it. "Actually, in a case like this, the longer you wait, the colder the trail gets. Memories become fuzzy. Witnesses, who might have made a connection to something or someone they saw that day, forget things that seem trivial at the time. It's better that the truth come out."

"All of it?"

She shook her head. "We don't disclose the details, but the conclusion of the investigation is inescapable."

Kelly let out a whoosh of breath. "I don't ever recall a murder in this town."

"Then you've been lucky," Chelsea told her friend.

The pregnant waitress came over. "Hi, Mayor. How are you?" She gave him a menu and told him about the dinner special, which he ordered along with coffee.

"You should drink decaffeinated coffee at night," Kelly informed him. "Caffeine disturbs your natural sleeping patterns. You probably don't get enough rest."

"Thank you, Doctor, for that advice."

Chelsea felt like kicking him for the sarcastic tone aimed at his sister. She refrained. Recalling the peace she'd felt after their lovemaking, she wondered why life couldn't always be like that.

Because those moments are but interludes, reststops along the highway of life, as one might say. Recalling their time together, she wryly admitted they hadn't been so restful, but there'd been contentment afterward—

"What's so funny?" Pierce demanded, looking grumpier by the minute.

"Life," she said softly.

Kelly laughed while he glanced from one to the other. "Women," he muttered.

"Yeah, we got you outnumbered, big brother. You'd better watch yourself," Kelly said.

He didn't respond to the teasing. Instead, his eyes on Chelsea, he said, "You'd better watch it. There's a murderer loose in the town. It's known that you were called in as a special investigator to work with Holt. Both your lives could be at risk."

The grin slipped from Kelly's face, to be replaced by worry. "Chelsea is alone in that cabin by the lake. Yours is the closest house, and it's a good distance away. The noise from the creek could cover up any sounds of struggle."

Chelsea gave her friend a smile. "I come from the city. That means I lock up every night."

"Locks," Kelly scoffed. "He could come through a window. What about a burglar alarm?" she asked Pierce.

"Hmm, we could run a line from the cabin to my place. All you'd have to do is push a button to summon help."

"That isn't necessary," Chelsea assured him. "From the evidence, it was a crime of passion. Those aren't usually repeated."

"Usually," Pierce echoed. "If a person has killed once, what's to prevent him from doing it again?"

Their food arrived, interrupting further discussion. A woman came in carrying a big, covered tray. A boy and a girl followed, each carrying a box. The owner of the diner rushed forward to help her with the load.

Chelsea watched them unload pies and cakes. The kids—the twins she'd seen at the lake yesterday—carried cookies which were put in huge bins behind the counter. A man entered, also carrying a box. It was filled with muffins of various kinds, she saw. They were obviously a family.

"Libby Adler, now Jessup," Kelly said, seeing her interest. "She and Marcus recently married. Those are Libby's twins from her first marriage. She was a widow and earned her living by baking for the diner."

"Marcus is probably as rich as Bill Gates. What's she doing still baking?" Pierce asked.

"She likes it," Kelly defended the other woman. "It's nice to earn your own money and not be dependent on a man for every penny."

"You feminists need to learn that men expect to support their family. They don't mind sharing the money they earn. As long as they get something in return."

He looked at Chelsea at that moment. Her insides squeezed into tangles like a ball of yarn after a kitten is through with it. The fire in his eyes was hot, consuming. It reminded her of the hunger that ran rampant between them when they dared release it.

"Ahem," Kelly said, amusement in the sound.

Chelsea pulled her gaze from his and focused on the meat-loaf special she'd ordered. She had to swallow around the tightness in her throat after chewing each bite.

Glancing at the family with the twins, she wished them a happily-ever-after existence. The woman looked young, in her twenties. Thirty-four wasn't old, but if she was going to have a child before she was ancient, perhaps she should check into adoption when she returned home.

A child without a husband?

She truly believed the family unit started with a man and a woman. Children needed both parents, if possible. Not that single-parent families couldn't be successful, she added, longing adding to the turmoil within.

"I'd like to have twins," Kelly said after the family had left. She grinned impishly at her brother. "You'll make a wonderful uncle. I'll let you baby-sit every Friday while Jim and I go out for dinner."

"Thanks," he said dryly. "Have boys. I'll teach them to fish and hike. We'll go camping."

"Girls like the outdoors," Chelsea said. "Why should they be left out?"

His gaze swung to her. "You're right. I should take girls hiking and camping."

The teasing flash of his smile stole her heart right away. She forced herself to breathe deeply until she found the inner well of quiet that had served her so well all her life, during her parents' divorce and the new marriages, the time when Pierce had told her he'd never intended a long-term relationship with her...

Pierce was aware that Chelsea had withdrawn to some internal place where she became an observer of what was going on around her, rather than a participant.

Kelly continued talking about the baby and their plans for it. She and Chelsea chatted and laughed, but he knew Chelsea wasn't there, not emotionally. It gave him an odd feeling to realize he knew her so well.

Why shouldn't he?

They'd been lovers for most of her last year in medical school. He, Chelsea and Kelly had often been a threesome on weekends. Except at night. That's when he'd wanted Chelsea all to himself.

Covertly studying her, he wondered why she hadn't married. She'd fulfilled her ambitions careerwise. Why wasn't there a man in her life?

Why shouldn't that man be him?

He was jolted, then intrigued by the question that leaped into his mind. Yeah, why not?

The question beat at him during the rest of the meal, the meeting he had that evening and on the drive home.

The lights shining through the cottonwoods along the creek reminded him that she was there, just beyond the creek...and that she'd welcomed him into her arms and bed at noon that day. Heaving a disgusted sigh at his musing, he parked in the garage and went inside.

Instead of turning on a light, he stood by the window and watched as the light went off next door. Chelsea had gone to bed. He ordered himself to do the same.

But he stood there, staring out at the shadows as if in a trance. He shook his head, denying the need that haunted him, remembering how long it had taken to get over her leaving eight years ago. Not that he'd been in love or anything like that. A man was just better off avoiding that kind of entanglement.

With this conclusion he went to bed.

An hour later he rose and pulled on jeans and jogging shoes, then walked out the door. Without thinking about his destination, he crossed the creek and lawn, then stopped at the screened porch on that side of the house.

"Chelsea?" he said, spying a ghostly figure on the wicker love seat.

"Yes."

"I thought you'd gone to bed."

"I did. I couldn't sleep, so I came out here."

He opened the screen door and entered, letting it slam softly behind him, then sprawled in a rocking chair, his legs stretched out, his hands jammed in his pockets. His feet were only a couple of inches from hers. Hers were bare. "I couldn't sleep, either."

"Are you worried about the case?"

He gave a snort of laughter. "The case didn't enter my mind."

"I've been thinking about it, about a lonely librarian who fell in love with the wrong man."

Pierce heaved a deep breath. "I've been thinking about us."

"There is no us," she reminded him.

Anger flared at her denial. He ignored both it and her refusal to admit to anything between them. "Maybe not, but there's an undeniable attraction."

She swung her bare feet onto the love seat and tucked them under her. An invisible shield seemed to surround her.

"You can't deny what happened between us today," he said in a husky voice.

"I'm not."

There was something stoic and resolute about her, as if she accepted the passion and, like a burden, was determined to bear it without complaint. She tugged at him, this woman who made her own way in the world and asked for nothing in return. But he knew she had dreams. She'd once shared them with him... her dreams and her passion.

Drawing a breath, he spoke what was on his mind. "I'd like to share that with you."

She'd been watching the moonlight on the lake. Now her head snapped around. "I don't think that would be wise."

He shrugged. "Probably not, but with you here in this cabin I won't be able to stay away. I don't think you would refuse to let me in."

The silence lasted an eternity. Blackness gathered within him, a void he couldn't explain.

"We can have this," he continued, "while you're here. When you return to Billings, it'll be over. We'll get on with our lives."

"And this will have been a pleasant interlude?"

"Yes," he said.

"We'll each go our separate ways when the time comes."

"Yes."

Again the silence. He let her think it over. He'd presented a sensible solution to their dilemma, so now it was up to her to see that was the best one. She could move in with him, then he wouldn't have to worry about her being over here by herself at night.

Finally she shook her head. "I don't think so."

The rejection was like a kick in the chest. He realized he hadn't expected it, not after their time together earlier that day. He stifled the whirl of emotions, froze them in ice until they stopped their fury.

"Fine," he said. "We'll play it your way."

He was pleased that he spoke with just the right mix of cynicism and amusement, good traits to cultivate with her.

Inhaling deeply, his common sense was momentarily shaken as the scent of her powder and shampoo and cologne enfolded him in an odd sense of peace and excitement, something he'd felt before with her, he recalled. He'd loved the scent of her eight years ago. It intrigued him now.

The quietness was in her. He wondered if it didn't express some sadness deep within. He didn't know.

"I'm not playing," she protested softly. "It's just that I think it's better not to start something that has no future. It seems…pointless."

"You didn't want a future before," he reminded her. "You had your career all mapped out. Nothing stood in the way of that."

She seemed puzzled when he reminded her of the cold facts. "I wanted to be a forensic pathologist, yes. It would have been foolish to give up a residency I'd worked for all my life."

"I agree."

"I wanted to ask you to wait for me." She laughed briefly. "I don't suppose women can do that. But I thought we could work something out. I thought… well, it doesn't matter now. Anyway, I'm not interested in a vacation fling, but thanks just the same."

Her words stung in ways he couldn't define. He muttered a good-night and retraced the path to his house. Before going inside, he paused, then shucked his jeans and shoes and headed for the lake. The cold water cleared his head.

Chelsea was right. There was no point in getting involved in a relationship that had nowhere to go.

* * *

Saturday morning Pierce asked Holt Tanner to stop by his office. "I want someone assigned to Chelsea," he told the lawman. "If there's a killer in town, he might look for an opportunity to get rid of our expert witness."

Holt gestured impatiently. "Why would he do that? She's already done the autopsy and turned in the report. If she disappears, we can call in someone else. What would he have to gain by getting rid of Dr. Kearns?"

"You can't tell what a warped mind might think. I want someone watching her place at night at the very least."

"Okay, I'll see what I can do," Holt agreed. "It isn't as if we have cops hanging around with time on their hands."

"Do the best you can," Pierce requested in a more reasonable tone.

The deputy studied him for a moment, then grinned and shook his head. "Sure thing, Your Honor."

Pierce hid his irritation until after the lawman left his office, then he smacked the desk in frustration. He was the one with a warped mind, worrying about Chelsea when neither she nor Holt thought it was necessary. He vowed not to intervene in the case again. Let the law do its work.

But what if the killer decided Chelsea could pinpoint him? The sheriff thought the personality profile would be a big help to their efforts if indeed the perp turned out to be local.

Pierce sprang from the chair and paced the mayoral office with its impressive rows of bookcases containing the history of the town reduced to minutes of city council meetings and ordinances passed over a hundred-year period.

Funny, a hundred years didn't seem a long time for a city, but a year out of a person's life could last forever.

A year. That's what he and Chelsea had shared. If after a year with him she'd wanted to leave, why the hell had he thought she might be interested in a couple of weeks?

He slammed out of the office after telling his secretary he'd be absent the rest of the morning. He drove to his house, then checked on Chelsea. She wasn't home.

Going to the deck, he spotted a lone figure, definitely female, a few yards up the shore. In the middle of the lake a man pulled on the oars of a fishing boat. Pierce watched for a moment. The fisherman seemed to be heading toward the woman.

"Chelsea," he yelled.

She stopped and looked back.

"Wait up." Jogging, he joined her on the walking path around the lake. "What are you doing?"

"Hiking around the lake."

He noticed the fishing dory had changed its course, heading back for the middle of the lake. "It's almost four miles in perimeter."

She glanced at him as if in reprimand for his snarling tone. "It's a nice walk." She strolled on.

He stayed with her. "I don't want you traipsing around by yourself. It's too dangerous."

She disagreed.

"I never realized you were so bullheaded," he muttered after a futile argument.

"There's no need for a watchdog. The perp is practical and calculating. Leaving a trail of bodies in his wake wouldn't be to his advantage."

"So, based on the flimsiest evidence, you've decided you have nothing to fear," he concluded.

Chelsea was aware of the fury in Pierce at her refusal of protection. Neither made any sense. When Holt had called and told her he was sending a man out, she'd laughed and told him not to bother.

She refrained from laughing now. Pierce was teetering near the end of his rope. She appreciated his concern even though she knew he felt it was his responsibility to watch out for everyone in town.

"You're a good mayor," she said.

"Huh," was his reply as he stalked along beside her.

Smiling, she added, "But a grumpy one. Really, Pierce, you don't have to worry about me. I've actually taken several courses in self-defense."

He'd been studying the lake. Now his head snapped around. "You've been in danger before?"

"Not really. But sometimes I was called out on a crime scene in the middle of the night. I thought I should be able to defend myself from muggers."

"Muggers," he scoffed. "It's murder that worries me."

"I know. It must be difficult to think that someone you know, someone that you perhaps speak to everyday or have a meal with or see at church, could be a killer." She gave him a sympathetic glance.

He was staring at the lake again.

"What is it?" she asked.

"Nothing. A fisherman. He's gone now. He left the boat near the swimming beach instead of returning it to the boathouse. I'll have to send a man to row it in."

She spotted the boat across the lake. "People can be so thoughtless."

But not Pierce. He was thinking so strongly she could almost hear the wheels turning. She felt his concern as a palpable thing.

"I'll be careful," she promised.

"I'm going to have a burglar alarm installed at the cabin."

"Please don't. I'll be gone in two weeks—" She stopped and considered. "Shall I go now? That would be simpler."

"No," he said. "You'll stay until we solve this."

Since the scowl on his face was so forbidding, she didn't argue. Besides, she wanted to stay. This was her vacation. She deserved some time off and a chance to rest and to consider her options.

Observing Pierce, she realized she could still say yes to his suggestion, ridiculous as it was. With a start, she also realized she was still thinking about it. She'd said no to him, but she hadn't said no to herself and the hunger that haunted her day and night.

"Pierce said he would pick you up," Kelly told Chelsea later that afternoon. "No sense in you both driving. I think bro is worried about you being alone, anyway. Let's indulge him on this."

Chelsea coiled the stretchy telephone line around her finger. "I really feel like an intruder on your mom's birthday dinner. Perhaps I should stay home."

"Nonsense. Mom is looking forward to seeing you. It's been three years since you stopped by after completing your residency. I had to twist your arm to get you here then."

Chelsea knew when to give in gracefully. "Okay. I'll see you shortly. What are you wearing?"

"Khaki slacks and a T-shirt. Don't come fancy. It's just family."

"Right. Here's Pierce, I think. Bye." She hung up and went to the door.

A car had stopped down the lane. She couldn't

tell what kind it was, other than a nondescript dark sedan. The driver stayed inside.

Probably a fisherman considering the best spot to catch the biggest trout, she decided, ignoring the hair that stood up on the back of her neck. Disgusted with the sign of fear, she gathered her purse and a jacket. With black slacks and a black, white and tan striped blouse, she was casual but dressy enough for a birthday celebration.

A clay pot of summer annuals was her gift to Kelly's mom. Another of dried flowers was for the hostess. With those at hand, she returned to the door.

The car was gone. Odd, but she'd sensed something evil there. Was it her imagination?

Tessa Madison, the psychic she'd met on a case, could tell the difference, but Chelsea wasn't sure if Pierce's worry hadn't influenced her. In fact, it probably had.

Shrugging off the spooky sensation, she clutched her purse when she saw his SUV on the lane. By the time he arrived at her front door, she was ready to go.

He opened the car door for her and stored the pots on the floor in the rear. "Thoughtful," he said.

She noticed the beautifully wrapped gift on the seat. "That package is too lovely to be opened. I always hate to mess up the paper when it's so pretty."

He grinned. "Mom says the same. But then, by the time we get to the cake and gifts, she's dying to see what's inside and can't wait to tear into it."

"How is she getting along?"

"Fine. Busy as usual with her church doings and volunteer service."

"It's nice that she'll be close by when Kelly has the baby. My mom spoils her grandchildren something awful, according to my sister."

He glanced thoughtfully at her before he turned onto Main Street, then onto Cave Springs Road where Jim and Kelly had bought a small ranch.

"Odd," he said, "but I think of you as being alone, as if you're an orphan. You don't mention your family very often. Why is that?"

She saw a deer lift its head and, chewing, gaze at them as they passed. "It's ordinary. My mom and stepdad have three grandkids from my two sisters on that side. My dad and stepmother have one grandson from their oldest son. He's divorced now. The younger brother isn't married."

"Two sisters, two brothers and four nieces and nephews. That's impressive. Kelly and I are falling behind, so my mom has told us."

Chelsea smiled. "She'll be glad to hear Kelly's news. Does she know yet?"

He shrugged. "I doubt it, or else I would have gotten a call to inform me it was time I married and reproduced."

At his wry laughter, Chelsea laughed, too. "Parents are all alike. Both mine worry about me and my lack of suitors. They think it's because of their divorce."

He slowed to a crawl. "Why is there no man in your life?" he asked, his voice going husky.

Because I never met another like you? Because you stole my heart? Because love once caused pain and I'm afraid to go down that road again?

"There really hasn't been time," she said, which was also the truth. "Being on residency call twenty-four hours a day wasn't very conducive to romance. When I started to work full-time, police departments all over the country were realizing the value of forensics. I was even busier."

"No long-term relationships?"

"No." Nor short ones, either, but she didn't say that. She'd dated, but it really hadn't interested her.

"It's the same for me. Being mayor and running a business take all my time." He turned onto the gravel road of the ranch. "A person in a small town has to be careful. See a woman twice and the town matrons have you nearly married and out the church door."

"It can be that way in the city, too," she told him.

They exchanged sympathetic glances. They were still smiling when Kelly greeted them at the house. "Out on the patio," she said. "Since we're having this heat wave, I thought we should take advantage of it and enjoy the outdoors as much as possible. That's a lovely package, Pierce. What did you get?"

"I'm not telling. You'll have to wait until it's opened to find out." He handed her a bottle of champagne. "You probably can't drink this, but you can join in a toast to the dear ol' gal."

"I heard that, young man," Mrs. Dalton called from the patio. "Come out here so I can smack your face."

"This is for your mom. These are for you," Chelsea told Kelly after he left them, handing her the pot of dried flowers. "You don't have to water them."

"Since she's never remembered to water a plant in her life, that shouldn't be a problem," Jim said, coming into the kitchen. He gave Chelsea a hug and welcomed her to their home. "I'll give you a tour later. We've made a lot of progress in remodeling. Only about forty years and we'll have the place shipshape."

Laughing, they went outside where Mrs. Dalton had indeed smacked Pierce. The print of her lipstick was still on his jaw. "Chelsea, it's good to see you again."

"And you. Many happy returns, Mrs. Dalton."

Mrs. Dalton gave Chelsea a kiss, too, and patted the glider beside her. "Sit here and tell me all your news."

Chelsea sat down and tried to think of something exciting. Her gaze settled on Pierce. "Well, I guess you've heard the news about the town librarian. That's the most exciting thing at the moment. In a terrible sort of way," she added.

"It's sad what people do to each other," Mrs. Dalton agreed, nodding regretfully. "But you're on vacation now. What do you think of the cabin and the resort? Pierce did a good job there, didn't he?"

"Mom," he scolded but with a resigned laugh.

She was undaunted. "Mothers can brag on their children. If I catch you doing it, though, I won't like it."

Kelly came out and leaned against her husband. He looped an arm around her, his gaze tender when he smiled at her. "Mom," she said, "we have an announcement."

Mrs. Dalton looked from her daughter to her son-in-law. Tears rushed into her eyes. "Oh, my," she said, going to them and throwing her arms around them both. "We're going to have a baby, aren't we? Is that it? A baby?"

"Yes, yes and yes," Kelly said. Then they all laughed and cried together.

"Here." Pierce handed his handkerchief to Chelsea.

She thanked him and dried her eyes, self-conscious about being sentimental about babies.

"Would you like a baby, Chelsea?" he asked out of the blue.

Heat flooded her face. "Yes. I'm thinking of adopting," she admitted truthfully. "Someday."

He studied her, his expression unreadable. "You'll need a husband."

"Maybe not."

"I forgot," he said with an edge to his voice. "You independent women don't need anything."

She refused to be put down. "That's right." She smiled at him, then put on an air of gaiety the rest of the evening. She oohed and aahed over Mrs. Dalton's birthday gifts—a dress and slacks outfit from Kelly and Jim, a porcelain figurine from Pierce to add to a collection. Mrs. Dalton was as enthusiastic about her gift of flowers as the other presents, which made Chelsea feel good.

On the return to the cabin, Chelsea realized she hadn't had to pretend. She'd had a good time. Glancing at her escort's profile as he guided the car along the moon-silvered road, she wondered what he would say if she were going to have a child.

Not that it was likely to happen. But she wondered....

Chapter Five

Sunlight played lightly across Chelsea's face Sunday morning, waking her from a sound sleep. She yawned and stretched, resentful of the early hour, especially since she hadn't fallen asleep until after midnight.

Too restless to laze around in bed for long, she rose and pulled on her bathing suit. The morning air was crisp, giving promise of cooler days to come. Soon, she hoped.

Setting her watch for the usual twenty minutes, she started her morning swim. Sunlight gleaming off metal caught her eye as she started into her first stroke. Standing, she studied the shadows under the trees down the lane.

A vehicle was parked there, almost hidden.

The hair on her arms stood straight up. Worried, she continued her swim, but ducked out of sight behind the deck at the water's edge on the return lap. She made her way through the trees until she was hidden from the vehicle by the cabin. Working her way around it, hiding behind trees and shrubs, she walked parallel to the lane until she could clearly see the SUV.

"Oh, for heaven's sake," she muttered when she realized who it was. She stalked over to the vehicle and yanked open the door. "What are you doing?"

The driver, who'd been sleeping soundly, stared at her as if she were an apparition. "Uh, watching the cabin," the young deputy said. "You're supposed to be inside."

"I take an early swim."

"Oh."

"Have you been here all night?"

"Yes, ma'am."

"Who sent you?"

"Uh, Holt put me on the stakeout. The sheriff didn't like it, but Holt said you might be in danger."

Chelsea's anger let up. She managed a smile. "The only danger is to my blood pressure. I thought somebody was stalking me when I saw your truck hidden in the bushes."

"No, ma'am, just keeping watch. There's a murderer loose in the town, you know."

He looked so earnest, the rest of her fury abated. "Since you're here, how about breakfast? If you'll get us a Sunday paper, I'll fix bacon and pancakes."

Grinning, he checked his watch. "I'm off duty now, so it should be okay. I'll be right back."

She returned to the cabin, rinsed off in a quick shower and dressed in blue shorts and a matching top. Tying a scarf around her damp hair, she went to the kitchen and put on a pot of coffee. When the young deputy returned, she had their meal nearly done.

"What's your name?" she asked, pouring him a mug of coffee.

"Gregory Smith. Everybody calls me Greg."

"I'm Chelsea. Shall we go out on the porch to eat?"

"Sure."

Carrying their plates, they went out on the screened porch. Birds were chirruping. A breeze ruffled the lake surface. The sun gilded the treetops in a soft gold patina. All seemed right with the world.

"I got the local paper and the Billings one. I didn't know which you liked."

"Good." She passed him the bottle of pancake syrup and picked up the local paper. LOCAL WOMAN MURDERED read the headline in bold capital letters. "Oh, great," she muttered.

Skimming the story, she saw the reporter didn't have a lot to go on, but the woman did know there were no powder burns around the wound or traces of gunpowder on the victim's hand as there would have been in a suicide.

Greg scooted his chair closer so he could read the article. "Holt's gonna be mad. Who told her about the powder burns and all?"

"That's the million-dollar question," she said. "Uh-oh, look who's here."

Pierce crossed the grass and joined them, coffee mug in one hand, newspaper in the other. "What are you doing here?" he snarled at Greg.

"I've, uh, been here since midnight—"

"What!" Pierce looked ready to leap upon the blushing young man and choke him.

"Holt sent me out to keep an eye on Chel—uh, Dr. Kearns. I'm off duty now," he added. "She invited me to stay for breakfast."

"You could probably use some food," Chelsea said to Pierce. "There's plenty in the kitchen. Why don't you fix a plate and join us?"

He gave her a scowl that would have melted an iceberg had there been one handy, then stomped into the cabin. By the time he returned, the deputy was finished.

The young man rose when Pierce thumped his plate down. "I'd better go. I have to file a report, then get some sleep before tonight."

"Thanks for your help," she called to his fleeing back. When he was in his truck and gone, she turned on Pierce. "You arranged for him to be here, didn't you?"

He shrugged and helped himself to the syrup. After pouring a generous portion over a tall stack of pancakes, he dug in. "These are good," he said.

She wasn't appeased. "I will not be spied on."

"It's for your safety." He bit into a crisp slice of bacon and munched while watching her.

"I'd be just as safe if left alone. Safer, in fact. It nearly scared me to death to know someone was lurking around the place this morning until I got close enough to see his uniform. Now I'll have to wonder if it's the police or the murderer when I see a man in the vicinity."

"You went down and checked him out?" Pierce practically roared. "Don't you have any sense at all?"

She narrowed her eyes and returned his glare. "And what should I have done?"

"Called me. I would have made sure it was safe for you to come out."

"I am not going to call for help like a…a ninny every time I see a car in the lane."

He didn't answer for a furious minute, then he grinned. "Okay," he said, "no more surveillance."

Chelsea was suspicious. "None?"

"None. I'll tell Holt to forget it. He doesn't have a cop to spare looking out for stubborn females, anyway."

"Fine." She studied Pierce's innocent expression as he calmly ate, his eyes scanning the article in the paper. "Why don't I trust you on this?"

He looked up. "Beats me. I'm as honest as the day is long."

"What happens after the sun goes down?" she asked with more than a trace of cynicism.

"Ah, that would be telling." He frowned. "Dammit, where did Liz get this information? She knows details from your report. In fact, she quotes it word for word in one place."

"I noticed," Chelsea said. "This Liz Barlow, does she have a relative in the sheriff's department?"

"Not that I know of, but there are probably connections between most families in the county. Only Holt Tanner has the actual copy of your report, and he's supposed to keep it under lock and key."

"Well, there's a leak somewhere in the department." She pushed her plate away, the food half-eaten. She was no longer hungry.

"Yeah. I'll talk to Holt. He must have talked to someone. Unless…"

She realized he was looking at her. "I haven't told anyone a thing," she protested hotly.

"Not intentionally," he agreed, "but did you say anything to Kelly? You were discussing it the other night in the diner."

"Only what you heard—that it was murder." A shiver ran over her all at once. "The cold finger of death touches more than one life in a case like this," she murmured, saddened by it all.

"Yes." He glanced at his watch and grimaced. "I have a conference call this morning with a couple of my managers. Here, take my cell phone in case you want to walk around the lake. Stay in plain sight. Don't go into the woods for any reason, even if you hear someone calling for help. Okay?"

Seeing the worry in his eyes, she didn't argue. She took the phone, checked how it worked, then laid it on the table. "Thanks. I appreciate your concern." She managed to inject sincerity in the words.

"I'll be over around nine tonight, if not sooner." He headed for the screen door.

"Tonight?" she repeated, trying to remember what was supposed to take place at that time.

"To spend the night."

"There's no spare bed," she reminded him.

"The sofa will do. If you won't take police protection, then you'll have to accept mine. You're on my turf now, Dr. Kearns. You'll do as I say."

She was still trying to marshal her arguments long after he left. Absently she carried the dishes inside and put them in the dishwasher, then straightened up the cabin. She vacuumed and dusted and scrubbed the bathroom, a chore she hated, then looked around for something else to do. A one-bedroom cabin didn't offer many possibilities.

Finally she collected a book and the cell phone, then went out to the deck. There she quickly glanced all around the lake, alert for any suspicious characters or actions.

"Ohh," she muttered when she realized what she was doing. Pierce was making her as paranoid as he was, about her safety.

After a while she relaxed. With the day came warmth and a sense of security. She fell asleep in the middle of the page.

* * *

Pierce finished the conference call with the men who managed the other two fishing/hunting resorts he'd built in the past five years. Each place—one near Missoula, Montana, the other in Wyoming—was earning a healthy profit.

One manager wanted to add a golf course similar to the one here at Rumor. He'd promised to think about it.

After reading over a couple of reports, then signing checks left the day before by the accountant, he finished up the paperwork and locked the desk. Since becoming mayor, he had to work in his own business affairs in odd moments.

The telephone rang before he could get away. He hesitated, torn between duty and desire.

The answering machine picked up the call. An irate citizen demanded to know what he was doing about keeping the residents from being murdered in their sleep.

"Everything I can and then some," he muttered, and went out the door. He quickly surveyed the scene.

Not a cloud dotted the sky, which was the blue depicted in picture postcards. A pleasant breeze wafted over the land, blowing down from the spectacular Beartooth Pass to the south of them. Several kids played on the beach or in the roped-off swimming area in front of the vacation cabins on the east side of the lake.

He scowled at the pastoral view, his mood as dark as a gathering storm. Someone was leaking information on the case, and he wanted to know who. He'd informed the sheriff and his chief investigator of that fact an hour ago.

First of all, he wanted the leak traced to its source. Second, he wanted some results, not assurances that they were doing all they could. Third, he wanted Chelsea safe and out of harm's way.

Perversely, he also didn't want her to leave Rumor. Not yet. There were issues to be resolved between them before she left.

Spying Chelsea on the deck, he cursed, then gave in to the need to check on her. As he drew closer, he saw that she was asleep. He stepped silently onto the wooden planks and leaned against the railing.

After checking all around for signs of danger, he simply watched her, an odd contentment seeping into his bones, soothing the turmoil from earlier.

Where the sun dappled her hair, the strands gleamed with gold and red highlights. She'd acquired a slight tan during her week at the lake. Her legs were long and slender, strong but delicately curved. One was crossed over the other and a flip-flop dangled from the strap between her toes.

Her face was peaceful in its repose. She looked young and vulnerable, as idealistic as she'd been when he'd first met her. He wished they could start over with a clean slate as of this moment. Maybe things would be different.

His heart thundered like a stampeding herd of buffalo. Worry and regret and other emotions rushed over him, leaving him baffled and uncertain of his motives.

Her eyes opened, and she spotted him. She glanced around the area, then back at him. "Keeping watch?" she asked, her manner amused, remote.

"No, just seeking some agreeable companionship. Know where I can find any?"

He liked the way her eyebrows shot up in surprise, then the drollness of her grin. He liked the suggestion of a dimple that formed at the corners of her mouth. He liked the soft line of her lips and the fact that her lipstick was gone. He liked…too damn much.

"Not around here," she said, no longer distant. She opened the book on her lap and returned to her story.

While she was engrossed, he continued his watch, noting the people who came and went on the other side of the lake as the morning wore on.

After a while Chelsea's head nodded. The book, a novel of lust and danger, the dust jacket proclaimed, fell to her chest. She slept again.

It came to him that she hadn't slept well since coming to the resort. That was hardly surprising. So far it hadn't proved a very restful time.

Pushing off the railing, he pulled a lounge chair close to hers and settled in it after another perusal of the landscape. He yawned, then let his eyes drift closed. A humorous thought crept into his mind. They were indeed sleeping together.

Okay, not together, but at the same time and the same place. Same thing, he decided and, grinning, dropped into a deep, peaceful slumber.

"Well, well, what have we here?"

Chelsea woke with a start. Kelly was standing beside her chair, her eyes, blue like Pierce's, were sparkling with mischief. In the chair next to her, Pierce sat up and pulled the back of the lounger into an upright position.

"Beauty and the Beast, napping like angels," Kelly continued. "I should have brought my camera."

"A polite person would have left them asleep and gone on about her own business," Pierce told his sister, but without much heat.

"Ah, but then you wouldn't have gotten this delicious treat I brought over for you. Brownies with walnuts. Yummy!" She took a big bite out of one.

"Hey!" Pierce made a swipe at the platter.

"You shouldn't have bothered," Chelsea said, smiling at their play.

"Actually, I didn't. I bought them at the diner. Jim and I wondered if you two would like to come over for supper tonight. I thought we'd do some trout on the grill, provided my lazy brother will provide the trout."

He yawned and nodded. "Sure. There's plenty in the freezer, I think. Help yourself."

"There is. I checked before I came looking for you." She set the platter on a low wicker table. "Come over about seven, okay?"

"I really should…" Chelsea tried to think of something she needed to do.

"No, you shouldn't," Kelly said with a mock frown. "This is your vacation, which officially starts today. We're going to celebrate."

Chelsea knew when to give in gracefully. After her friend had left, she sighed and reclined in the lounge chair, her eyes on the peaks beyond the lake. "It's so peaceful here."

"Yeah, when people aren't killing each other." He stood and paced the deck. "Sorry, I shouldn't have said that."

"It's okay. I know you're worried."

He propped a hip on the railing and watched a couple rowing about the lake, their inexperience bringing laughs from their friends on shore.

Turning back to her, he said, "I don't want the killer to be a local person. I want him to be an outsider, someone passing through, a simple robbery gone wrong. We had a lot of tourists in town for the last weekend of the Crazy Moon Festival."

"Maybe it was one of them." She knew it wasn't.

He shook his head. "It's someone we know…and trust. Someone we would never suspect. After all, we certainly didn't suspect Harriet had a lover. I've tried to pick out a man in the community who might qualify, but there isn't one who comes to mind. I suppose that's an insult to Harriet."

Chelsea sympathized with his dilemma. "She was a secretive person. She chose to hide her wealth and her personal life from everyone."

She sat upright and put the marker in her book. Laying it on the table, she offered him a brownie, then took one for herself after he did. She glanced at her watch. "I slept most of the morning."

"You were tired. It's been a busy week. You probably haven't slept well since you arrived."

Her eyes met his. It took an effort to look away. She was confused by the concern she witnessed in those blue depths. "Why are you so worried?" she asked. "Do you know something I don't?"

He shook his head. "It's just a feeling...like something's wrong, but I can't put my finger on it."

She recalled the chill she'd experienced while near the deceased woman's chair. "Murder is what's wrong," she said gently. "A lone woman, an unborn child, an eruption of anger that leads to violence and death. It leaves everyone unsettled and unsure about their safety in a community that normally leaves its doors unlocked."

"That's changed. The hardware store sold out of dead bolts and padlocks as soon as rumors of murder started circulating. I asked the sheriff to put more men on the case, but he says he doesn't have any to spare."

"Holt has done everything there is to do at the present. He did a very good job gathering evidence. What there was of it. Colby Holmes is trying to help, too."

"From what I hear, he's been more of a nuisance than anything else."

"He spread the word about the murder. I think that should have been acknowledged from the first."

"The sheriff and I agreed that we shouldn't jump to conclusions. That's why we wanted your expertise. I was right to send for you. We would never have known about the pregnancy otherwise. It had to have been her lover."

When he shot a questioning glance her way, Chelsea realized he was still baffled by the case. "Yes, I think it was her lover. Find the father of her child and you'll find the killer."

"He didn't really care about her or the baby, did he? He just didn't care."

Chelsea realized Pierce was trying to understand that fact, that his personal idea of manhood was the protection of women and children and he couldn't see how another man could harm those who trusted him.

Something in her went warm and liquid. She wanted to wrap her arms around him, to comfort him and tell him not all men were as honorable as he was.

Controlling the impulse, she said, "He cares for his own image more. His position in society is more important than any other feelings he might have."

"I live with the thought that we may never know who he is." His manner was introspective, dark with the specter of death hanging over them. "I find that idea impossible to tolerate."

"It outrages our sense of justice. Unfortunately, right doesn't always prevail. I've learned that since I started my job. It's hard when you see criminals walk away and you know they're guilty."

"Yeah. Let's walk around the lake," he suggested.

She sensed his restlessness and the frustration of feeling helpless in a serious situation. "You're not responsible," she told him. "It isn't your job to solve the case. You have a community to run."

He smiled grimly. "And to keep safe."

When he reached for her hand, she didn't pull away. For the next hour they strolled the paths around the lake edge. At the main lodge of the resort, they went inside for lunch.

"I'll give you a tour after we eat," he promised, seeing her curious glances at the lobby and the shops that lined corridors to each side when they went to the restaurant.

"I'm glad you got to build this place," she said sincerely, admiring the soaring architecture. "It was your dream, you once said, to build a paradise. You did it."

"Did I?" he questioned softly, holding a chair for her at a table covered in white linen.

She cast him a surprised glance over her shoulder.

"I've found paradise is more than a place." His smile was sardonic. "I still have to find my Eve to go in it."

Her breath caught so that she could hardly speak. "I'm sure Kelly will be glad to help."

"Oh, yes. She and Mom are ever on the lookout for the perfect female to fit in our little Eden. So far, no luck."

Chelsea ignored the throb of blood through her body. She hadn't been that woman eight years ago. She wasn't going to try out for the part now.

Chapter Six

Pierce worked on the account books during the rest of the afternoon. The three resorts, the golf course, the real-estate office in town, all were doing well. Since becoming mayor, he'd found he didn't have to do all that much about overseeing operations. His managers were quite competent to handle the details.

Finishing up, he locked the file cabinet, checked the desk for anything he'd forgotten, then headed for the shower. It was nearly time to pick up Chelsea.

His body tightened at the thought. He couldn't deny he was eager to see her. He'd looked at the clock every half hour while taking care of business.

So what?

An unbidden smile tugged at his mouth. Sure, he wanted to see her. He wanted a repeat of Friday.

Which wasn't likely, given her resentment at being watched, he added in all honesty. However, as long as she was in his neighborhood and under his care, she'd follow orders regarding her safety.

He drove around to her place. "Ready?" he called out upon reaching the cabin's rustic door.

"Just about. Come on in."

He crossed the screened porch and entered the living room. Chelsea's scent drifted on the hot summer air, enclosing him in a light fragrance of perfume and powder. He recognized the balsam from her shampoo and the clean, minty odor of the soap she used.

Gripping the back of a dining chair, he waited out the spasm of need that rocketed through him. When she came out of the bedroom, he was under control once more. Barely.

"I'm ready." She picked up her purse and checked its contents, then snapped it closed and slung the strap over her shoulder.

Tonight she wore a summery dress of black pleated silk that left her arms bare and teased him with an enticing plunge to a point between her breasts. She carried a black shawl over one arm.

Glancing at his fresh jeans and white shirt, the sleeves rolled up on his arms, he said, "You're pretty fancy tonight."

"Do you think the dress is inappropriate? I can change to slacks—"

"You're fine." He grabbed her arm and hustled her out, heading for his sister's house, a sense of déjà vu running through the scene.

It was more than the fact of the birthday party last night. Somehow it seemed he'd done this with her in the past. He hadn't. Although she'd visited his sister after her training, he'd stayed out of the way. Three years ago he'd been in Missoula when she came to visit.

He was glad when they got to the ranch. Being in the closed SUV, having her within arm's reach, tempting him with her subtle scent, was almost more than he could take. It was going to be a long two weeks, he decided, unless she accepted his offer to move to his house and his bed.

Glancing at her quiet pose as she studied the passing scenery, he was sure that wasn't going to happen.

He parked in front of the old ranch house and escorted Chelsea around to the patio where the grill was going and trout were sizzling. Rolls were in the warming bin. Baked potatoes browned to the side of the fish.

"I'll go help Kelly," Chelsea said after greeting Jim with a hug. She went inside.

"Here," Jim said, and handed over a beer.

Pierce took a cool drink. It didn't help his mood.

"You look about as happy as a three-legged mule in a mile-long race."

Pierce managed a half smile. "Troubles," he said.

Jim nodded, his cheer fading. "The murder?"

"Chelsea," Pierce admitted. "I shouldn't have insisted she come down here. The autopsy could have been done in Billings as well as Whitehorn."

"You think she's in danger?"

He shrugged. "Have you ever sensed something but couldn't put your finger on it? Like there's something you should put together but can't?"

Jim was silent while he turned the trout and basted them with a butter sauce. "Follow your hunch," he finally advised. "Sometimes your senses pick up signals that don't register in your mind. I've spent a lot of time in the woods, and I've learned to trust my instincts, especially where danger is concerned."

"Holt Tanner doesn't think Chelsea has anything to worry about."

"Maybe not. But maybe she does. There's a killer in the area. Until we know who he is and have him locked up, I want Kelly to be careful, too."

"You don't think—"

"No," Jim interrupted, "but I don't want her trusting everybody she meets the way she usually does. That's all."

Pierce nodded. His sister had a tendency to butt into other people's lives. She told parents how to raise their kids and scolded them about their own health and about setting examples for their families. He hadn't thought about her being in danger, though.

"Hellfire and damnation," he muttered.

"Yeah, it drives me crazy, too," Jim said. "I grew up in Jersey where you belonged to a gang or else. Even then your life could be wasted for no reason. Maybe you just happened to get in front of a stray drive-by shooting. I came out West to get away from all that."

"You can't get away from people and their foibles."

"I've learned that. I've also learned to grab happiness and hang on to it with both hands. For me, that's Kelly."

Pierce's attention was drawn to the kitchen as Kelly and Chelsea laughed at something. In a few minutes they came outside with plates and silverware and napkins.

"I'm starved," Kelly told her husband. "Are the fish about ready?"

"You're always starved nowadays," Jim said with a grin at Pierce. "Pregnant women," he muttered.

Pierce thought of the coming baby. He'd be an uncle, which he found sort of fascinating. His gaze went to Chelsea, and he pictured her carrying a baby in her arms. The scene was so real he would almost swear he'd actually seen it.

"Pierce, you're staring," Kelly said, breaking into his intense introspection. She gave him a sisterly grin, as if she knew exactly what he was thinking.

"Sorry." He took the platter from her and held it while Jim dished up the trout and potatoes. Kelly brought the rolls, and they all adjourned to the patio table.

"This is a lovely place," Chelsea commented. "Up here on the bench, you can see the whole town. Over there, where the lights are, that must be Whitehorn."

"It is," Jim told her.

"Beyond that, the mountains seem to go on forever, one peak after the other. I've always loved that sense of eternity. A city seems very here and now, but the mountains are timeless."

Pierce watched the setting sun backlight the peaks to the northwest of them. The Crazy Jane Mountains, they were once called, after a woman, supposedly insane, who had lived there long ago. Now they were referred to as the Crazies.

His gaze went to Chelsea. He sensed a longing in her and wondered what she wanted that she didn't have.

The answer came to him instantly. Chelsea really wanted a family. She'd been an outsider in her parents' new families, now she wanted a child of her own.

An odd sensation grabbed at his chest. He hadn't done a lot of thinking about a wife and kids, but he'd had assumptions about them. They went with the package that life handed out. A man met a certain woman, they married, the kids came along. Presto, a family.

At thirty-six, he wasn't sure things were going to fall into place quite so easily. Maybe a person had to work at it. If that's what one wanted from life.

For the rest of the evening, he considered this question. Kelly and Jim set a fine example of a happily married couple, but they'd had their tense moments. Life was an on-going process....

He realized Kelly was looking at him. "What did you say?"

"I asked if you'd installed a burglar alarm at Chelsea's cabin," she repeated.

"No. But it's okay," he said at her worried frown. "I'm going to stay over there at night."

An instant silence enclosed them.

"On the sofa," he added.

Jim grinned skeptically. Kelly laughed aloud. Chelsea shot a glare his way, looking stubborn. Okay, so he'd blown that one. He shrugged. "I am," he told her.

She stuck her nose in the air. "That's not necessary."

"Maybe not, but Kelly'll feel better. We don't want to upset her, do we?" He gave Chelsea an innocent smile.

"Ha," she said.

Oddly, he relaxed and enjoyed the rest of the evening. Later, arriving at the cabin, she didn't invite him in. He followed her, anyway. "I meant it about staying the night."

She rounded on him, but not in anger. "I'd rather you didn't." She folded her arms across her chest in a defensive posture.

Embers burst into flames inside him. She was as tempted by their mutual desire as he was. The need was in her eyes. Mixed with it was despair as she fought the temptation.

He wanted to take her into his arms and smother the worry with hot kisses and hotter caresses. He took one step forward, then his sense of fair play intervened. She had to come to him of her own free will, because it felt right to her, not because he overcame her scruples.

"I'll stay on the couch," he promised. "There's passion between us, but I won't take advantage of it. When you come to me, I want it to be done openly and free of doubt."

"Is that the way you feel?"

"I have some doubts. Like you I question the point of starting something with no future."

Her eyes moved over his face as she considered. Finally she nodded and, murmuring a good-night, went into the bathroom and closed the door. He caught the news on the television while she prepared for bed.

When the bathroom was free, he did the same. Coming out, he spotted sheets, blankets and a pillow on one of the easy chairs. With a wry smile at the closed bedroom door, he made up his bed on the sofa.

Surprisingly, he fell asleep easily and spent a peaceful night on the makeshift bed.

* * *

Chelsea woke early Monday morning. She listened but couldn't decide what had awakened her. Seeing the closed door, she wondered if Pierce was still on the sofa.

After slipping into her bathing suit and coming into the living room, she saw he was. He slept with one arm over his head, the other tucked under the blanket, which was pulled up to his chin. He looked vulnerable lying there, his face as innocent as a boy's.

Her heart warmed, sending a rush of blood through her body. She'd missed him. All these long years there had been a void inside that nothing else could fill.

Or maybe she hadn't tried hard enough to fill it, she chided, going outside. She crossed the deck and climbed over the railing in order to jump down into the shallow water along the cove, then waded into a deeper part of the lake.

She began her morning routine, stroking strongly in a line parallel to the shore, swimming between the tree she used as a landmark and the deck. Only she and a lone fisherman out on the lake in a boat interrupted the solitude of the morning.

For some reason she felt peaceful and secure in this little corner of paradise—

"Get out of the water," a shout broke into her musing. "Chelsea, get out of the water."

She stood and looked back. Pierce pounded down the shoreline at a dead run. He whizzed past her and dashed into the water. Her mouth agape, she watched him grab the fisherman, who had rowed to within a few feet of her, and drag the man out of the dory.

The man struggled as Pierce dunked him under the surface of the lake and held him there until the struggles stopped.

"Pierce! What are you doing?" she yelled, coming out of her shocked trance. "Let that poor man go. You're drowning him." She tugged at his arm.

"I'll let him go when he tells me what he was doing."

"He can't talk with his face underwater," she felt bound to mention.

Pierce cautiously let the man up, but maintained a grip on his arm, which he twisted behind the man's back.

"Call him off, lady," the fisherman pleaded, shaking the water from his face. "I didn't do anything."

"What were your intentions toward Chelsea?" Pierce demanded, giving the man an additional shake that sent the water flying in all directions.

"None. I swear."

"Pierce, please, what are you doing? Can't you see you've scared him senseless? Let him go."

"Only if he answers my questions."

"I will," the man promised.

Pierce loosened his hold but kept up his threatening glare. "Start with your name. You got any ID on you?"

"In my pocket. Can I get my wallet?"

Pierce nodded.

Chelsea kept an eye on them while the fisherman very slowly retrieved his wallet and handed it over. Pierce snapped the soggy leather open and checked the driver's license. "Wallace Ledbetter," he read off the name, then checked the photo. "Yeah, that looks like you."

"It is." The man sounded more sure of himself. "Who the hell are you?"

"I'm the owner of this land," Pierce told him. "You'd better have a good excuse for being on it."

The man drew himself up, looking as indignant as a wet hen. "I'm a paying guest. The penthouse suite at the lodge," he added. "I'm thinking of suing."

"Go ahead. I'm still thinking of drowning you. What were you doing stalking another guest of the resort?"

"I was trying to catch a huge rainbow trout I spotted the other day. He stays in a hole just on the other side of those rocks." The fisherman pointed over his shoulder. "I've spent three days scouting out this place. Now I'll have to start over. After all that thrashing about, the rainbow has moved to the next county by now."

Chelsea felt as irritated as the resort guest obviously did. "Pierce is very sorry he interrupted your fishing," she said, acting on an impulse to bedevil him as he was doing to her. "Aren't you, darling?"

she asked sweetly. "He was worried about me," she explained to the man.

"Because of that murder you had here?" the man asked, looking interested.

"Yes. There's a lunatic in the area. You probably should pack up and leave," Pierce suggested, eyeing the man with cold disdain.

"Don't be silly, darling," she scolded. "Why should he cut his vacation short? With you to protect the guests, I see no reason to worry. You should give the poor man an extra week at no cost. After all, you did nearly drown him."

The man smiled broadly. "Well, thanks. Can I have a rain check for next year? My vacation is over this week."

Pierce narrowed his eyes at Chelsea. She widened hers in a totally innocent expression. "Sure," he said without glancing at the resort guest. "I'll see that you get a gift certificate before you leave."

"All right!" the man said enthusiastically. He waded to his boat and climbed in, water dripping from his clothing and sloshing in his shoes, which he pulled off. Nodding, he rowed off toward the buildings on the other side of the lake.

Chelsea heaved a relieved breath. "All's well that ends well," she told Pierce. "Let's go in. I'm starved."

He waited until they were inside the cabin. "Darling?" he questioned softly. "Darling?"

"Well," she hedged, "the man obviously saw us come out of the same cabin. He must have thought we were, uh… Anyway, I thought it best to pretend we were…" She couldn't think of an appropriate word.

Pierce took one step closer. "When you play with the devil, you have to pay his dues." With that warning he reached for her. "You owe me, *darling.*"

Alarmed, her heart beating like sixty, she stepped back, but was unable to break his grip on her arm. "For what?"

"For all the worry you put me through. For saving you from an unknown fate. For a night of dreams that has stirred my appetite to ravish you to unbearable heights."

"Don't…don't you dare," she warned, seeing the intent in his eyes.

"Or what?" he challenged. "Tell me the consequences."

She tried to think of something that would deter him. All she could think of was how good his arms would feel, of how solid he would be against her, how warm…

"I need to take a shower," she said in a hoarse whisper.

"An excellent idea." He swept her into his arms. "An excellent idea, indeed."

To her indignation, her arms closed around his neck and refused to let go. "Pierce, we can't. We shouldn't," she managed to say.

"We can and we should," he said with great certainty. "A hot shower will fix us right up."

He dumped her into the tub, flicked the cold water on full force, then walked out of the cabin. Shivering, she raced to the window in time to see him leap the stepping stones over the creek, then jog to his house.

Her spirits topsy-turvy like a raft in a stormy sea, she returned to the bath. With warm water sluicing over her, she shook off the disappointment and, oddly, the tears that collected behind her eyes.

It really was better to maintain a distance, but there for a minute—okay, she admitted it—she'd given in to madness. She wanted him. She wanted his kisses, his exciting touch. Most of all, she wanted forever.

"And forever is something he isn't offering," she murmured, lathering her hair.

If she could just remember that, she'd be all right. As long as her heart wasn't involved, she could handle the attraction. Simple. Now that she had it all figured out, she would relax and enjoy her vacation.

Chelsea was reading again when the cell phone rang. It was Holt Tanner, the chief investigator on the case.

"I need your help," he said. "Can you come to the Martel cottage, like now?"

"Sure. I'll be right there," she promised. "Is this official or unofficial? I'm in shorts and a T-shirt."

He hesitated. "Unofficial. I'll see you there."

She mulled over the call while she grabbed her purse and car keys, then slipped on sandals to replace the flip-flops and headed out. The deputy had sounded a bit odd, his words clipped and tense. Hmm.

At the victim's house, she parked behind two vehicles, one the deputy's cruiser, the other belonging to the sheriff. A news van was parked behind a pickup on the street in front of the cottage.

Inside, she heard an altercation. A woman's voice was among the deeper male tones, each apparently trying to shout the other down.

"Dammit," Holt was saying as Chelsea walked in the door. "I'm going to arrest the whole bunch of you."

"I have a right to be here," Colby Holmes, the deceased woman's nephew, declared. "I have a copy of Aunt Harriet's will. I'm the executor of the estate. I'm taking an inventory to see that nothing has been removed."

"No one has a right to cross a crime-scene tape. That includes you." Holt glared at an attractive woman and a man with a video camera, who was filming the whole thing.

The woman ignored Holt. "Sheriff, is it true that Harriet Martel was four months pregnant when she was murdered? Do you think this had anything to do with her death?" She held a microphone under the sheriff's nose.

Dave Reingard pushed the microphone aside. "Where the hell did you get that information? It's classified."

A gleam appeared in the reporter's eyes. "So she was pregnant. Who was the father?"

Holt took the woman's arm and stuck his nose in her face. "Who was your informant? I'll get an injunction from the judge if I have to," he told her.

For a second she looked defiant, then she shrugged. "I got an anonymous tip. A phone call. I checked it out," she quickly added. "The caller was at a pay phone in Whitehorn. I'll give you the number, but I doubt if he left prints."

"He?" Holt questioned.

"I think so. The voice was disguised as a whisper, but I think it was a man."

Holt studied her for a minute, each of them holding his or her ground, then he pushed the reporter past Chelsea and out the door. He beckoned for the cameraman to follow.

"Are you the state investigator on the case?" the dauntless reporter asked, holding the microphone out to Chelsea. "Are you the forensic pathologist the mayor asked the state to send down?"

Holt, disgust plain on his face, gently but firmly shoved the nosy woman off the porch, then turned to the man.

"I'm leaving," the cameraman declared, hurrying out the door but continuing with his filming.

"I'll have to confiscate that." Holt took the camera and removed the film.

"I'll sue," the woman warned, furious now.

"And I'll arrest you if I even see you in the neighborhood again," Holt shot right back. "Dammit, Liz, you know better than this."

She looked momentarily ashamed, then the fury returned. "Well, *he* was here." She nodded toward Colby.

Chelsea realized the woman was Liz Barlow, the reporter who had copied phrases from the official report almost word for word. She seemed to be good at ferreting out the facts…with a little help from a secret pal.

After the news crew left, the cottage seemed strangely quiet. Holt glared at Colby. Colby glared at Holt. Chelsea glanced at the sheriff, who had remained mostly silent during the scuffle. The sheriff was looking at the room.

"I told you to stay out of it," Holt finally said to the nephew.

"Yeah? When are you going to make an arrest?" Colby demanded. "Have you looked for the killer?"

"Let the law handle this, son," the sheriff said, his manner sympathetic and soothing. "The wheels of justice grind slowly but steadily. Dr. Kearns here is helping Holt research the case."

Colby turned on her. "Have you found any clues?"

She gave him a noncommittal perusal. "We're checking every possible avenue. With all the traffic on the scene, though, any remaining clues have probably been lost."

The young man had the grace to look abashed at her mild accusation. "I want to help. My mother is upset that nothing seems to be happening."

When Holt opened his mouth, the sheriff held up a hand. "Let him stay," he said. "What can it hurt?"

Chelsea noted the glances exchanged between the chief investigator and his boss.

"Can you show me exactly what you think happened?" the sheriff requested of her.

She nodded after glancing at Holt, who shrugged as if giving up on police protocol. "She was slapped first, hard enough to send her to her knees...about here, probably." Chelsea indicated a spot at the archway into the alcove. "There's a bruise on her hip to indicate she hit the chair railing before falling."

The sheriff checked out the chair railing. "She was alone when the intruder broke in. She must have been pretty frightened," he said, looking sad.

"Not then, I don't think," Chelsea said. "There's no sign of forced entry or a scuffle before the blow. She knew the man. She let him in. I think they had a serious quarrel and that he wanted her to get rid of the baby. He slapped her. That's when she became frightened. She turned, maybe to run from him, but he hit her on the back of the head, hard enough to stun her and cause a concussion."

"How do you know that?" Colby interrupted.

"Contusions in the skin, fracture lines at the base of the skull," she told him, "dealt after the slap."

"Then he shot her?" the sheriff asked.

"He put her in the chair." Chelsea pointed toward the easy chair next to the reading table in the living room.

Colby crossed the room and stood by the chair, his gaze fixed on it as if he were watching the scene. "He shot her here. Just like that." He snapped his fingers.

"She probably said something," Chelsea suggested. "It triggered his rage even more. Maybe she again refused to get rid of the baby, or perhaps she threatened to expose him as the father of her child—"

"Do we have proof it was the father?" Sheriff Reingard asked, obviously surprised. "There're no signs...well, she didn't date as far as anyone knows. I was thinking she could have wanted a child and gone to a sperm bank. There's one in Billings, that fertility clinic I read about."

Colby muttered an expletive to show what he thought of this idea.

"Well, she was, ah, somewhat secretive," Reingard said defensively. He turned back to Chelsea. "So what happened next?"

"He took the threat seriously," she continued. "Miss Martel was semiconscious, maybe murmuring about what she would do. The perp was standing to this side of the chair. He took out the gun—"

"From where?" Holt interrupted.

Chelsea looked around. An old-fashioned sideboard stood next to the wall. Three small drawers lined the front. "From there." She opened the nearest drawer. Other than the green felt lining, it was empty.

The hair rose on her neck.

She opened the other two. Each held an assortment of odds and ends usually found in such places. The glaring emptiness of the one drawer was silent affirmation of the scenario she painted for the men.

"He removed the gun and shot her as she rested in the chair." Chelsea enacted the scene with an imaginary weapon. "He wouldn't have had to take a step. He simply lifted the gun, swung it around and fired. That works," she said to Holt. "The angle of the bullet entry was from this side and above her head, about four feet away."

The sheriff closed the three drawers, his face solemn as he sighed. "So then he decided to make it look like suicide by putting the gun into her hand? Wouldn't her prints have already been on it?"

"He had wiped the gun clean before he thought of staging a suicide," Chelsea explained. "He panicked for a second, then started thinking it through. He pressed the gun into her hand, then let go so it would fall naturally."

"But it was too late," Holt added. "There were already too many things wrong with the scene. He should have opted for a robbery gone wrong."

"Who knows what he thought," Reingard muttered, bending over the chair. "There's not much blood for a close-range shooting."

"The slug stayed inside the skull," Chelsea told him. "I recovered it, as I explained in my report, and asked for a ballistics test." She looked at Holt.

The deputy nodded. "The ballistics report showed the gun found on the floor was the one that killed her."

"Aunt Harriet didn't own a gun," Colby insisted. "Find the owner of the twenty-two and you'll find the killer."

"We've run a check. There's no record of the weapon registered in the state or with the FBI," Holt said.

Colby went to the chair and nudged the sheriff aside. "This was her favorite spot. She read every night sitting right here." He picked up the book on the table and flipped it open to the bookmark. "She was reading this book."

Chelsea's heart went out to the nephew. He was hurting, and there weren't any words to comfort him. She couldn't assure him they would find the murderer.

"Look at this," Colby said, staring at the back cover of the book. "It looks like a name...or initials—"

"Let me see that!"

Holt grabbed the book, and they all crowded around to stare at the nearly indecipherable prints on the back. "Written in blood," he said.

"Aunt Harriet's blood," Colby said in a stricken voice. "She was trying to leave us a clue."

The sheriff traced over the letters. "That looks like an *H* and an *I*. The third letter could be almost anything—an *N*, no, an *M*."

"Or an *R*," Holt said. "Not much of a clue."

"But it's more than we had before," Colby said furiously. "How did you miss it?"

Chelsea felt sorry for the deputy as the sheriff and the nephew looked to him for answers.

"I don't know," he said slowly, "but I'll find out. If it takes the rest of my life, I'll find out. The investigating team was supposed to fingerprint everything."

"The book was dusted." Chelsea pointed out the residue. "What happened to the report on this?"

No one had an answer.

Chapter Seven

Colby Holmes followed Chelsea out to her car after the sheriff left. Holt had taken charge of the book. A fingerprint was discernible on the cover, along with the scratched initials, and he was going to check it out personally. He was still inside the cottage, going through everything again.

Chelsea thought it was useless. The murder trail was growing cold and apparently going nowhere fast.

"Wait a minute," Colby requested when she started to get into her car. "I have a question."

She studied the handsome rancher and former rodeo star. In his late twenties, he exuded energy. He moved like a big cat on the prowl, an impression of animal strength and power about him. Worry creased twin lines on his brow. "Yes?"

"Those letters, initials, whatever they are," he began, then paused. "They were written in blood, weren't they?"

It was her turn to hesitate. Finally she nodded. "Tests will have to be made, but yes, it looked like blood."

"Aunt Harriet's?"

She shrugged.

"Or the killer's?" he persisted.

"Well, unless she injured the person, it would be hers. She was bleeding from the slap. Her bottom lip was split."

He clenched his fists. "God, that makes me see red—he hit her and then shot her, a defenseless woman. She was a quiet person and kept to herself, but she wasn't mean."

Chelsea considered something she'd thought of before. She laid a hand on Colby's arm. "Listen, about three years ago, I briefly met a psychic on a case. She was able to supply a clue that led the police to the perp."

Colby gave a skeptical snort.

"No, really, she did. I'm not saying it would work this time, but maybe she could help. I met her in Chicago, but she lives up this way, I seem to recall. I could ask the detective who was on the case."

"Other than ol' Winona Cobb, who lives near Whitehorn, I've never heard of any other psychics around here. What's her name?"

He looked so scornful, Chelsea was tempted to tell him to forget it. However, there was the case to be solved. "Tessa Madison. Is the name familiar?" she asked at his startled frown.

"Yeah. If it's the same person, she owns a shop near here, one of those New Age places. Mystic something, or something Mystic. I can't remember."

Chelsea was delighted. "That must be her. Where is the shop? I'll stop by and tell her to expect you—"

"Don't bother," he said, heading for his truck. "Why don't you and Holt take the book to her? Maybe she'll get a vision and presto, all will be answered."

If Chelsea'd had a thick book in her hands, she might have been tempted to hit him with it, she decided wryly, watching Colby drive off. Men thought they knew everything.

She left the crime scene. On Main Street, she decided on lunch at the diner. First she'd check with Kelly and see if she was available.

"She'll meet you at twelve-thirty," the receptionist reported after checking with the doctor. "Order the special for her if she's late. It doesn't matter what it is. She likes everything they serve."

Laughing, Chelsea put the cell phone in her purse and headed for the diner. The cheerful, pregnant waitress directed her to a table. The woman wore a wedding ring, Chelsea noted and was glad.

When she was seated, Chelsea also noticed a man at the counter watching the waitress, his gaze tender. She instinctively knew this was the husband. When the waitress refilled his coffee mug, a special look passed between the two, confirming her conclusion.

Her heart gave a painful lurch. She'd arrived in town a week ago today and, as she'd feared, it had been a troublesome seven days. Her emotions had run from doom and gloom to irrational joy. There was just no sense to it.

Holt Tanner entered the diner, stopping her introspection. He spotted her and came over. "The sheriff thinks we ought to question Louise Holmes. She's Colby's mother and sister to the dead woman. Would you mind coming with me?"

"Not at all, but why? She was questioned the first day. What are we looking for?"

He sat down opposite her and leaned close. "Harriet's will leaves everything to Louise. Perhaps the sister knew of Harriet's money and decided she wanted it now."

"I doubt that," Chelsea murmured.

Holt grimaced. "I do, too. From digging around, I've found both sisters inherited a nice nest egg from their parents. I guess that's how Harriet got started investing. Besides, Colby did well on the rodeo circuit. He would see that his mother didn't lack for anything."

Chelsea agreed.

"However," Holt continued, "he is the executor of the will and stands to inherit everything from his mother since he's the last of the family. The sheriff thinks we should pay more attention to him, too."

Chelsea shook her head. "I'm sure it isn't him," she said in nearly inaudible tones. "He doesn't fit the profile. He's too volatile, for one thing, too involved to stop and think things through, the way the killer did."

"I think you're right." The deputy yawned and rubbed a hand over his face. "Colby can be a royal pain in the butt, but he isn't vicious. I'd stake my reputation on that."

"When should we go see his mother?"

"Stop by my office after you finish with lunch. We'll go then. If something else hasn't come up."

"What about the book and the blood?" she asked.

"It's on the way to Whitehorn to be analyzed. Want to bet it's Harriet's blood?"

She shook her head. "I think so, too. Unless we can figure out what she meant by the letters, we're stumped."

"Yeah. What a mess." He waved the waitress off when she offered him a menu and, nodding at Chelsea, left the diner.

Chelsea glanced around. Several pairs of eyes were on her, speculation rife in them. She realized she and Holt had been whispering, their heads almost touching as they talked.

Well, that should add an interesting tidbit to the rumor mill. She signaled the waitress and ordered for herself and Kelly with the hope that her friend would arrive soon. For some reason she felt exposed and very vulnerable sitting there alone.

Kelly and the food arrived together.

"Hi. You're just in time," Chelsea said. She studied her old friend. "What's wrong?"

Kelly sighed. "One of my patients miscarried this morning. The couple had wanted the baby so much."

"That's sad."

"Umm-hmm," Kelly said. "Like us, they waited until they were established in their careers and had a house. Maybe that's a mistake."

Chelsea thought her friend looked discouraged, although her tone had been cheerful. "It's hard not to become anxious, isn't it?," she murmured in sympathy. "We're in our thirties now. The clock seems to be ticking faster."

"Do you think about having children?" Kelly asked, her gaze curious. "You could try in vitro fertilization."

"Actually I'm thinking of adopting," Chelsea admitted after reminding her friend of the medical reasons she was unlikely to carry a child.

"I've always thought of you as the dedicated career woman, and that was the reason you'd never married and started a family." Kelly was silent for a moment, then added, "Pierce was devastated when you went back east for your residency."

Chelsea's heart did a gigantic lurch at this news. "Surely not," she said when she could trust herself to speak. "He never wanted a long-term relationship."

Kelly shot her an incredulous look. "He would

have married you in a heartbeat if you'd said the word." Her voice carried a trace of anger.

Chelsea didn't take offense at her friend's defensive attitude about her big brother. "Well, he never said so," she said lightly. "Anyway, we were so busy those last two months, what with exams and graduation and packing. There was no time for anything else."

Kelly frowned as if she would say more, then apparently changed her mind. She glanced at her watch. "I have to hurry. The office is rushed today. In fact, we're busy enough for another doctor to join the staff. If you know anyone who's interested."

Her innocent expression didn't fool Chelsea for a minute. Kelly was determined to play matchmaker for her brother and her friend. Glancing out the window, she spotted Holt Tanner arriving at his office.

"I've got to hurry, too," she said. "I have a meeting with Holt this afternoon."

"Are you interested in him?" Kelly demanded.

Chelsea had to laugh. "Only as an associate on this case."

"Good."

"Kelly," Chelsea warned softly, "don't expect miracles while I'm here. They aren't going to happen."

"Pierce sent for you," Kelly reminded her.

"Because of my job."

"Huh, the coroner in Whitehorn could have performed the autopsy. He didn't have to send for you.

Even if he doesn't realize it, he wanted you here. And you wanted to come," she finished triumphantly.

Chelsea held up her hands in surrender. She'd learned not to argue with a friend as stubborn as Kelly.

"I'm out of here," Kelly said. "Lunch is on me." She laid some bills on the table before Chelsea could protest and hurried back to the medical office.

Chelsea considered entering the practice with her friend. It was tempting, but she'd chosen her field long ago. She knew her own strengths. Investigating cases, having a hand in solving them, that brought her great satisfaction.

Enough for the rest of her life?

She struggled with the question and knew the answer. Work wasn't enough. There was a void to be filled. A child, she thought, gazing at the pregnant waitress. That's all she needed to complete her life. Really.

Louise Holmes was a softer, plumper version of her deceased sister, Chelsea observed when she and Holt Tanner arrived at the house. The woman rose from a patio chair on the tidy front porch and waited at the steps, the leaves from two huge oaks shading her face.

"Hello, Louise," Holt said in an easy manner.

"Holt," the woman replied. She gazed at Chelsea. "The doctor who did the autopsy," she said when Holt had introduced the two women.

"Yes," Chelsea said. "I'm sorry about your sister."

Tears glistened in the other woman's eyes, but she held her composure. "Thank you. It was sad, shocking, actually. Please be seated." She gestured toward the chairs. "Can I get you anything to drink?"

Holt answered for them. "No, thanks. We can't stay long. We just want to go over a few things with you."

After they were seated, Louise asked, "Have you found out anything?"

"Nothing new," the deputy said. "Would you mind going over your dealings with Harriet the past few months?"

The sister locked her fingers together. Chelsea saw they were trembling, but her gaze was straightforward as she asked, "What kind of dealings?"

"Did you notice anything different about her?"

"Like what?" Louise seemed truly perplexed.

Holt cast Chelsea an appealing glance. "Did she seem nervous or apprehensive to you?" she asked, taking over the interrogation.

"No. Well, there could have been something…"

Holt and Chelsea waited, but then Louise shrugged and shook her head.

"Did her habits change? Did she visit you regularly, then stop?" Chelsea continued the probe.

The sister thought it over, then slowly nodded. "Yes, that's it. That's what changed. We had dinner together every Sunday, either here or in town. A few months ago that changed. At first she would call and cancel at the last minute, which wasn't like her. Then, after a couple of months, she said she was busy and would call when we could get together again. I thought it was because of the planning for the Crazy Moon Festival. She was on some committee."

Holt took out a notebook. "Who was on it with her?"

"I don't know. The mayor's office should have a list." She looked directly at Chelsea.

Chelsea squirmed in the hard wooden chair and wondered if everyone in the county knew Pierce had stayed at her cabin last night. No, no. How could they? She was being overly sensitive. She managed an encouraging smile.

Louise Holmes smiled back, and Chelsea could see where Colby had gotten his charming looks. His mother was pretty when she relaxed a bit.

"She didn't mention the pregnancy?" Chelsea asked.

A spasm of pain marred Louise's features. She closed her eyes briefly, then looked again at Chelsea. "Never. Not once. She could have told me. We're...we were sisters. Colby and I are—were—her only living relatives. We would have helped, if we'd known."

"Helped?" Chelsea probed.

Louise raised her hands and dropped them in her lap in a helpless manner. "If she'd wanted to go away and have the child, I'd have gone with her."

"What about if she'd decided to have an abortion?"

"I'd have stood by her decision, but she would never have done that," Louise said with conviction. "She might have arranged for an adoption into a good home...no, she would have kept the child."

"You're sure?"

Louise nodded. "She didn't show a lot of outward emotion, but she loved children, loved reading stories to them and watching them discover the wonder of life." Tears filled her eyes and spilled over this time.

Holt shuffled uncomfortably as men did when women wept. Chelsea dug a couple of tissues out of her purse and handed one to Louise, keeping one handy for herself as her own eyes smarted. They talked a few more minutes, then she signaled she was ready to leave.

"Where were you the night of the lunar eclipse?" Holt asked suddenly, taking both women off guard.

"In town. Colby drove me in for the final night of the logging competition. We stayed for the concert."

"Was your sister with you?"

Louise shook her head. "She said she had things to do. I assumed she meant for the festival, but now I realize she must have been meeting someone." Her eyes filled with tears again. "Her killer."

A silence ensued. Chelsea felt the heaviness that thoughts of death imposed on the living. She also concluded that Louise Holmes hadn't murdered her sister.

"Can you think of anyone who had any type of quarrel with Miss Martel over the past few years?" she asked as gently as she could. "Sometimes people carry a grudge a long time. It festers, then erupts if an opportunity presents itself."

Louise shook her head. "Colby asked me the same. I've thought and thought on it. Harriet didn't make close friends, but she didn't make enemies, either. I know for a fact she helped people."

"In what way? At the library or personally?" Chelsea continued her line of questioning.

"Well, personally. She was something of a feminist—"

Holt gave a surprised snort at that.

"She was," insisted the sister. "She thought women should be able to support themselves, even if they were married. They shouldn't depend solely on men to take care of them. She said that was why a lot of women were trapped in bad marriages. They had nowhere to go and no confidence in themselves. She thought that was terrible."

"So you think there were women in town that she helped? Did she mention any names?"

Louise shook her head at Chelsea's probing. "I don't know anyone specifically, only that she was upset on behalf of some woman whose husband was a bastard, to use her term. Harriet rarely used strong language," the sister said with an apologetic glance at Holt.

When further questioning elicited no new information, Chelsea thanked the older woman for her cooperation. She and Holt started across the lawn.

"Do you think you'll catch him?" Louise called out.

Chelsea, noting the anxious expression and grieving manner, hadn't the heart to discourage her hopes. "I'm sure the culprit will be found."

"Ha," Holt said under his breath and held the door open for Chelsea to climb in.

In the police SUV on the way back to town, Chelsea spoke, "We have another suspect."

"Yeah? Who's the first one?"

"The lover," Chelsea murmured, her thoughts converging as she studied the facts. "There could have been an estranged husband."

"Harriet wasn't married." Holt was clearly impatient with this line of reasoning.

Chelsea ignored him. "I mean, what if Harriet helped someone, an abused wife who came to the library seeking refuge, and helped her get away… gave her the money to leave town…and the husband found out. He'd blame Harriet for his wife leaving him. Maybe he came to her house and demanded to know where his wife was. Naturally Harriet wouldn't tell him."

"She'd probably give him a lecture about doing right and insist that he attend an anger management class," Holt said. "Harriet didn't mince words when she was angry."

"That's probably what set her murderer off. She wouldn't back down and give in to his demands." Chelsea thought some more, then came back to the lover and father of the unborn child. "Did Harriet stop seeing her sister because of the demands of the committee work or those of the mysterious boyfriend?"

"The boyfriend," Holt said without hesitation.

Chelsea squinted against the brightness of the afternoon sun. "It's a rare person who keeps every part of her life secret. You know what I mean?"

"No."

"Even the most reticent person confides in someone—a friend, a family member, a priest. Has that been checked out? Did Harriet go to church? Did she belong to any clubs?"

"The American Library Association," Holt said dryly. "She went to church over in Whitehorn. We checked that out. She hadn't attended in several months." He exhaled in an exasperated huff. "She was the exception that proves the rule. She confided in no one, neither family nor friend."

"Or foe?" Chelsea suggested. "She told her lover. It infuriated him."

Holt hit the steering wheel in frustration. "Who the hell is he?"

Pierce smacked the arm of the deck chair with an open palm. "Who the hell could it be? This town is too nosy for anyone to hide an affair for long. Someone had to have suspected something."

Chelsea nodded absently, her thoughts on the conversation with Louise Holmes and her conclusion about the reclusive librarian having more than one enemy. She'd just informed Pierce of this new twist, but added that she was still betting on the boyfriend.

"After all," he continued, his tone changing, "it's already all over town that you and Holt Tanner are a hot item."

"What?"

"That got your attention," he said in satisfaction.

"Holt and I are working on the case. Doesn't everyone know that by now?"

"Apparently you seemed pretty intimate at the diner during lunch. Later you were seen going out of town in Holt's truck, then you returned over an hour later and spent the rest of the afternoon in his office…behind closed doors, or so it's rumored."

"Oh, for heaven's sake. We went to see the victim's sister. Does everyone think we were out parked like a couple of kids sneaking off to lovers' lane? Honestly, small towns are a pain." She glowered darkly at Pierce.

He grinned lazily. "I like to see you with your dander up. Your eyes flash and your lips get all pouty with disapproval. Your cheeks become charmingly pink."

She gave him a glare that should have shut him up.

He laughed softly, with an edge of cynicism. "I would be jealous—"

"Jealous," she said incredulously. "Of what?"

"Of Holt. Except I know how dedicated you are to your career," he finished.

"You've mentioned my career before. Why is it okay for a man to devote himself to his career, to ignore his family and put his goals ahead of everything else, but not for a woman to do the same? Answer me that."

"You're right. I'm out of line with my philosophy about men and women working together and sharing responsibility. Call me old-fashioned."

"I prefer mule-headed. If responsibility was shared equally, there'd be no problem, but family matters always devolve to the female. Every study shows the woman handling most of the duties in marriage."

"I'd be willing to share," he said, his gaze roaming the lake and the vicinity around the deck. He checked his watch. "Time to turn the chicken."

Chelsea watched him, her mood wary, as he opened the lid on the barbecue grill and turned the chicken breasts over, then basted them with sauce. She'd been surprised to discover dinner being prepared when she'd arrived at the cabin after an afternoon spent in Holt's office, going over the known facts and trying once more to come up with a face to match them, only this time that of another woman's estranged husband, someone who had a temper and was known as a wife beater.

Men. It was no wonder more and more women chose not to marry the louts.

"Why don't I trust this act of neighborly kindness?" she asked aloud while he refreshed their margueritas from a tall pitcher.

He laid a hand over his heart. "I'm crushed at your doubts." His grin was pure devil and then some. "Actually I'm carrying out orders. Kelly said she'd beat me with a broom if I didn't treat you nicely."

"Kelly has dreams of us marrying and me going into partnership with her. Our children would be cousins and play together as best friends, and we'd all live happily ever after." Chelsea sighed in exasperation.

"Would it be so bad?"

She was startled by the serious tone. He didn't smile when she met his eyes. "I don't know," she said truthfully. "I've never thought much about it."

After he'd made it clear long ago that he had no interest in a permanent relationship, she'd blocked those ideas from her consciousness. Her dedication to learning all she could about forensic techniques had been commented on more than once during her residency. It was all she'd had to fill the lonely hours of her days and nights.

She turned from his gaze. To the west, the setting sun highlighted the peaks in glorious shades of brilliant red and orange and gold, the result of the usual summer forest fires adding tons of debris to the air.

"Behind every lovely illusion," she murmured, "lurks a harsh reality. Harriet Martel discovered that in a very painful way."

"It's difficult to think of Harriet having romantic illusions," Pierce admitted, closing the grill and coming to the railing where Chelsea stood. "She seemed to have a stern outlook on life."

"Everyone has dreams," she said without taking her eyes from the twilight sky. However, she was aware of his heat as he stood close. Her heartbeat seemed to become louder.

"Have you fulfilled all of yours?"

She inhaled slowly, deeply, then shook her head. "I want a child. I'd like to adopt a baby, but that may be impossible. There's a long waiting list."

"What about an older one?"

"I've thought about that. Older children often have special needs. I worry that as a single parent I might not have enough time. I'll have to continue to work."

"There's no possibility you could have a baby?"

His chest brushed her shoulder, causing her skin to burn. She moved away unobtrusively. "Actually I could, but it would be the merest luck if everything came together just right and the embryo found a place to attach."

"Hmm," was all he said.

She found herself mesmerized by the fathomless darkness of his eyes as he studied her for a long minute. She was aware of each place his gaze paused—her eyes, her lips, her throat, which was suddenly tight and achy.

When he suddenly turned, she was disappointed and relieved at the same time.

"Dinner," he announced.

She rushed to hand him the platter, then went inside and brought out the pasta salad she'd prepared upon arriving home and discovering what he was doing. As twilight turned into deep dusk, they silently ate and listened to the calls of the night creatures on the summer air.

Chelsea lifted the hair from her neck after finishing the meal. "That was delicious. Thank you for preparing it. I'd already decided against cooking. It's just too hot."

"The weatherman says there's no break in the heat. The fire near Missoula is out of control."

"Kelly said you had a resort over there. Is it in danger?"

"Not yet, but it could be if any more fires break out."

"Maybe they'll get a shower soon."

Pierce stood. "I hope so. Let's go inside. The mosquitoes are coming out."

They took care of the dishes, then settled in front of the television to catch the news. No rain was forecast for the state, but the fires were contained. That was good. They watched a movie, then she rose to prepare for bed.

Pierce stood, too, and blocked her path. "About that child you want," he said softly.

A shiver rushed over her like a sudden cold shower.

"I'd be glad to father it."

She was speechless.

"But there's a condition."

"What?" Her voice came out a breathless wheeze.

"Marriage. You would have to agree to marriage if you became pregnant. I don't believe in having children without providing them with the security of a family."

"Oh."

He let her go. "So think on that and let me know." He walked to the sofa and spread out the sheets and blanket without glancing her way again.

Chapter Eight

Chelsea looked at the clock beside the bed. It was ten minutes later than the last time she looked at it, which was to say, five after twelve. She closed her eyes and ordered them to stay that way.

They did. For another five minutes.

Sighing in disgust, she flung the covers off and swung her legs over the side, searching around with her toes until she found her fuzzy slippers. Heading for the kitchen, she perked up as she remembered the ice cream she'd bought at the grocery when she'd arrived. She hadn't sampled it yet, and Rocky Road was her favorite flavor.

"What's happening?" a deep voice inquired.

Chelsea whirled from the fridge, a hand going to her heart. She spotted Pierce standing in the doorway between the living room and kitchen. "You scared me," she accused and turned back to the task at hand. "I'm having a dish of ice cream. You want some?"

"Yeah."

She was supremely aware that he wore jeans, but no shirt or shoes. His torso was bronzed by the sun. Wiry chest hair cast an intriguing shadow across his chest and ended in a dark line leading from his navel and disappearing behind the waistband of the jeans.

She gulped and fixated on getting two bowls from the cabinet, scooping out the ice cream and adding spoons, then setting his portion on the counter nearest him. Taking her treat, she went out on the screened porch and sat on the glider, her feet tucked under her.

Pierce followed and sat in a wicker chair.

"Why isn't it cold at night?" she murmured, aware of the stillness of the air and the heat that hung over the land even at this late hour. "It's supposed to be cold in the mountains."

"Global warming," was his answer, delivered in a grouchy tone.

She shut up and took a bite of ice cream. It crunched delightfully between her teeth, releasing the flavors of chocolate and nuts and marshmallows.

"What the hell is the crunchy stuff in this ice cream?" he wanted to know.

"Dung beetles."

A silence followed, then, "Very funny," he muttered.

"Don't ask if you don't want the answer." Satisfied that she'd scored one for her side, she relaxed and savored each cold, delicious spoonful of the dessert until she'd scraped the bowl clean.

"Here."

Pierce thrust his half-full bowl into her hands and set hers on the side table. He settled in the glider with her and set it into motion. After the briefest of debates with herself, she shrugged and finished off his bowl, too.

"Ah, that was good. If people had all the ice cream they could eat, the world would be a happy place."

"Ice cream diplomacy," he said sardonically. "You should write the president and tell him about it."

Undaunted by his attitude, she said, "Maybe I will." She set the empty bowl into the other one, licked the spoon and put it there, too. She checked the corners of her mouth with her tongue.

"You missed a spot," he told her.

She licked her mouth again. "Where?"

"Here."

Before she could react, he leaned close and, with the merest flick of his tongue, touched a spot on her chin just below the right corner of her mouth. A fierce sensation ran under her skin, causing her to gasp aloud.

"Pierce," she started, then couldn't think of exactly what she wanted to say.

"Kiss me, Chelsea," he murmured. "I'm hungry for the taste of you."

"Passion is foolish." She mentally groaned at how prissy she sounded.

"I know. Indulge me in this," he requested softly, his breath playing havoc along her cheek as he planted kisses there in barely felt caresses.

For a second she resisted, even as hunger flowed through her in red-hot waves of molten desire. Then her arms closed around his neck and locked into place, refusing to let go.

This was Pierce, her first, sweet, passionate love, the man of her dreams and fantasies.

"I want you," she said, and laughed at how simple the words were and how easy they were to say.

He stared deeply into her eyes, a question in his. Still smiling, she nodded.

"No regrets come morning?" he asked, his voice a husky rumble coming from deep within, its nuances like the earth-shaking murmur of a volcano before it erupted into fiery rivers of liquid rock.

"No regrets," she assured him.

"Good. I've been dying to do this."

Sliding his hands under her pajama top, he cupped her breasts and held them as if they were the most delicate treasures in all creation.

"You make me feel…special," she whispered, pressing her face into his shoulder. "Everything seems new and wonderful."

"It was always this way with us," he reminded her. "I loved touching you…feeling the smoothness of your skin, like satin, but warm. Hot," he corrected, then laughed.

His laughter touched her in ways she couldn't name. Tenderness washed over her, accompanied by a rainbow of other emotions too deep to identify.

Their kisses filled the void in her to overflowing. She ran her hands over his chest, sides, back, shoulders, into his hair, along his jaw, over his throat.

"Magic," she said. "You were always magic."

"Not me. You," he contradicted. "You're like a spirit who can appear or disappear at will. I'm never sure if you actually exist or if you're a moment's fantasy."

When he lifted her, she swung her legs across his thighs and settled in his lap, their minds and bodies in tune as if there'd never been a time of separation.

"Get rid of this," he demanded, bunching the pajama material in his fist.

"Yes."

The gathered cotton top was quickly tossed aside. He wrapped her in a close embrace. She reveled in the warm contact, the tensile strength of his muscles.

"Not enough," he said, kissing her a thousand times. "It's never enough."

He rocked forward and stood, lifting her into his arms at the same time. Feeling his way through the dark interior of the house, he carried her to the bedroom and laid her down. He paused with his hands on his jeans.

"Stay," she said.

That was all the invitation he needed. Quickly getting out of the confining denim, he then stripped the pajama bottoms from her, smiling when he saw they were fashioned like men's boxer shorts. She was all woman, the eternal female...and his.

For this moment.

"It doesn't matter," he murmured, sitting on the edge of the bed and covering her breasts with his hands.

"Wh-what?"

He liked the tiny catch in her voice and the way she rose to his caresses, pushing against his palms as if she, too, couldn't get enough of the touching.

"Tomorrow," he told her. "Tomorrow doesn't matter. There's just the here and now. And us."

She sat up and wrapped her arms around his shoulders. With her lips pressing steamy little kisses along his collarbone, she whispered, "Let's make the most of it."

He heard her laughter, but also the echo of sadness, as if she saw beyond this enchanted hour to another time, one only dimly perceived by him. He tightened his grip, suddenly knowing she was going to run from him like a latter-day Cinderella, desperate to be gone before the stroke of midnight.

"You won't disappear on me again," he told her. "Not this time."

Chelsea thrilled to the passionate fierceness of his embrace and to the hunger that fed it. Mixed with the desire was a gentleness that brought tears to her eyes as he bent and kissed her breasts, then licked along the valley between them and up to her throat before returning to her mouth with his devouring kisses.

"Not tonight," she agreed, but she knew nothing was forever. "Kiss me," she demanded, feeling the desolate emptiness of tomorrow already creeping close. "Kiss me now."

Caught in the tide of passion, she forgot reality and basked in the fire, then the sweet glow of their joined heat until she finally fell asleep, limbs entwined, her heart content.

Pierce arrived late at his office the next morning. "What day is this?" he asked the secretary. His desk calendar was still on Friday.

"Tuesday the ninth."

"Thanks." He flipped to the correct day. "I don't have any meetings today. Will wonders never cease?"

"Uh, actually the sheriff wants to see you and Dr. Kearns as soon as possible. I haven't been able to reach her this morning."

The sense of well-being evaporated. Pierce picked up the phone. "She's probably hiking around the lake. I'll see if I can contact her. Set up the meeting."

He got Chelsea on the cell phone and told her of the sheriff's request.

"I can be there in thirty minutes."

"Hold on." He checked with the secretary. "Reingard will be here at ten," he told Chelsea.

"I'll see you then."

Pierce hung up and swung his chair around so he could view the scene outside. The town looked peaceful, tucked into a fertile valley with a creek at each end, both eventually running into the Yellowstone River and finally into the Missouri, the Mississippi, then the Gulf of Mexico.

A sense of the continuity of life gripped him. At one point during the night, he'd wondered if he and Chelsea had made a child.

For a moment he felt a oneness with nature, an awareness of his own immortality reaching backward in time to his ancestors and forward through the offspring he might have. At that instant conception seemed not just possible, but inevitable between him and Chelsea.

The phone rang with a jarring staccato. He answered at once, his body tightening at the thought that Chelsea might be calling.

"There's a pothole right in front of my house that hasn't been fixed in six months," an irate citizen told him.

Reality snapped back with a vengeance. He grinned and reached for a pen and notepad. "What's the address?"

Chelsea wore her favorite cool mint-green slacks and top to Pierce's office for the meeting. She'd roused when he'd quietly left that morning to go to his place and get ready for work. "It's early," he'd said. "Go back to sleep." Then he'd kissed her and slipped out.

She paused in the corridor, willed herself to act in a normal manner when she faced him, then entered the outer office.

"Dr. Kearns," the secretary greeted her warmly. "The mayor is expecting you. Please go right in. Would you like a cup of coffee?"

"No, thank you." She went into the other office. The door immediately closed behind her and she was swept into a pair of masculine arms.

"Hi," Pierce murmured just before his lips came down on hers in a breathless kiss that sent her thoughts whirling.

After releasing her, he smoothed her hair, gave her an approving once-over, then grinned.

"Dr. Kearns," he said in formal tones, "I'm so glad you could join us."

"Us?" She glanced around in alarm.

"A figure of speech. The sheriff isn't here yet. I made fresh coffee. Would you like a cup?"

She saw the office was equipped with a sink, tiny refrigerator and coffeemaker hidden in an alcove with folding doors. "Uh, yes, that would be fine."

A knock sounded, then the secretary opened the outer door and announced the sheriff and Deputy Tanner.

"Come in, gentlemen," Pierce invited. He told his secretary to hold all calls, made sure everyone was comfortable, then took his place behind the desk.

"I assume this is about the Harriet Martel case?" he said, looking at the sheriff.

The sheriff sighed and rubbed a hand over his face. "Yes. Our latest finding didn't pan out."

"What finding?" Pierce cut a glance at Chelsea, who lifted and dropped her shoulders slightly.

"The initials on the book. Tell them the results, Holt," the sheriff ordered.

The deputy looked gaunt, the lines in his face more heavily scored. He wasn't sleeping well as the murder occupied his thoughts day and night, she diagnosed. Time was passing and he wasn't any closer to solving the puzzle of the missing lover.

"The blood on the book belongs to the victim," Holt told them. "So does the thumbprint."

Pierce muttered a curse. "What about the letters?"

Holt shrugged. "I've run a computer check on the ranchers and homeowners in the county, also the registered voters roster, looking at last names starting with an *N* or *M* or *R*. None have initials matching *H* and *I* for first and middle names."

"There's no question on the first two initials?"

"No, those are pretty clear."

"So what's next?" Pierce asked.

The sheriff spoke up. "I'm going to put the case on the back burner. We don't have enough people to keep an officer on it full-time."

"It's only been what…?" Pierce peered at his desk calendar. "…ten days since the lunar eclipse. Isn't that giving up a bit early?"

"We're not giving up," Reingard said coolly. "The case isn't closed. Holt will remain the chief investigator, but he has other duties to attend to."

Pierce wasn't put off by the sheriff's manner. "Like what? Investigating who stole those frozen chickens from the grocery last month?"

Holt hid a grin while Sheriff Reingard frowned, anger evident in his narrowed eyes. Pierce calmly met the lawman's hard gaze, his expression neither hostile or angry.

For the first time, Chelsea realized how exactly right he was for the mayor's job. He had a small kingdom to oversee, its safety and welfare his first concern. He brought humor and compassion to the office, but he also expected people to do their job and get results.

The sheriff unexpectedly turned to her. "Dr. Kearns, what's your opinion? Does the case warrant keeping a man on it full-time?"

She had no choice but to deliver an honest assessment. "Unless there are new leads to follow, we seem to be at a dead end. Deputy Tanner should keep the investigation on his active list—after all, it is murder we're talking about—but I doubt it will take up all his time as the situation now stands."

Pierce nodded when she looked his way. "Holt, you're the investigator. What's your opinion?"

The deputy appeared discouraged. "I'm looking into a couple of new things—people in town that Harriet might have helped in some way."

"How?" the sheriff demanded skeptically.

"Money, I think," Holt said. "She withdrew large sums a couple of times during the past few years. I've asked the bank for a detailed printout of her account, including copies of checks. I want to see how she spent her money and who it went to."

"She was the most secretive woman I ever met," the sheriff complained. "Who knew she had all that money squirreled away like a miser? She made the Library Board give her a big raise last year."

"She hadn't had one in three years," Pierce reminded the other men. "It was overdue. A person should receive a fair salary for value given."

"Tell that to the voters," Sheriff Reingard said ruefully, bringing a smile to Pierce's face.

"There is one other thing," Holt said as the meeting drew to a close. "Holmes is going to hire a psychic."

The sheriff looked mystified, then amused. "A psychic? Is she going to read his future in some tea leaves?"

"He wants to bring her out to Harriet's house and let her look around."

The sheriff was on his feet in an instant. "Absolutely not!" he said furiously. "There's been enough traffic through there. If any evidence existed, it's probably already been destroyed by Colby and his poking around, not to mention Liz Barlow and her crew." He glared at Holt as if it was all his fault.

"They crossed the yellow tape," Pierce reminded the sheriff, then glanced at Holt. "Why weren't they arrested?"

"The crime-scene guys had already checked the place out, so supposedly there was nothing to destroy. Besides, someone had leaked details to Liz. It had to have been someone in the department. I put all that in my report."

"Have you checked the leak?" Pierce asked the sheriff.

"I'll put someone on it," he promised grimly.

Chelsea decided she was glad she had no reason to run afoul of the sheriff. He looked ready to shoot anyone who crossed him at the moment. Murder was not a happy matter.

"What do I tell Colby?" Holt asked. "He's the executor of his aunt's estate. Does he proceed with closing it out? He'll have to have access to the house and all her records, which are closed by court order at present."

Chelsea observed as Pierce and the deputy waited for the sheriff to make the decision. Now that Colby was going to hire a psychic—presumably Tessa Madison, although he had mentioned some other woman— she saw no reason for her to go by the woman's store and talk to her. In fact there was nothing to hold her in Rumor. She should go.

"The house is off-limits for now," Reingard decided. "I want to go over the evidence myself before we give up. You can release the body for burial, though." He checked the time. "I have to go."

"Me, too. I've been assigned to handle the complaint desk the rest of the week." Holt nodded to her and Pierce, gave his boss a half salute and left.

Chelsea prepared to leave when the sheriff did, but Pierce asked her to stay. She settled back in the chair.

"What do you think?" he asked when they were alone.

"About what?"

"The nephew. The psychic. The deputy. The sheriff. Pick one," Pierce suggested. "God, I'm tired of this whole thing. Are most cases like this? If so, how do you deal with the frustration?"

"Few cases are solved in which the perp is a stranger who is passing through, but most domestic crimes, such as this one, are done by people known to the victim."

"Notably husbands or boyfriends," Pierce muttered.

"Exactly. Miss Martel's murder fits all the classic details for crimes of passion."

"Except the boyfriend seems to know how to cover his tracks perfectly."

"Yes. He's mature as well as cunning. He can think in a crisis situation."

"I'd like to get my hands on him," Pierce said direly, then shook his head, dismissing the thought.

"How about lunch? I know a place near Whitehorn that's nice. We can play hooky the rest of the day."

He looked so taken with the idea of escaping the town and its problems Chelsea didn't have the heart to refuse. "All right," she said, also feeling a need to get away from troubles and unending questions with no answers.

Excitement began to build in her. She tried to browbeat it into submission, but nothing worked. Being with Pierce was too alluring.

"You're quiet," he said once they were on the road.

"I'm wondering about Colby Holmes and the psychic." She told him about working with Tessa Madison once. "That was one of my first cases in Chicago. I knew she was from Montana, but I didn't realize she was right here in town."

"I don't know about being clairvoyant or whatever, but she has a shop of some kind. I think she sells crystals and, um, beauty bath stuff, you know, to make you relax."

"Aromatherapy and herbal remedies," Chelsea supplied. "They're the latest cure-alls."

"Maybe I should go in for a consultation," he said, giving her an oblique, sardonic glance.

Chelsea couldn't hide her surprise. "Why?"

"I think my heart is going to be broken soon."

She could only stare at him in confusion.

"You're thinking of leaving," he said as if this explained everything.

Carefully, slowly, in case she fell right apart, she protested. "You wouldn't notice if I did."

"Oh, yes. I'd notice." He pulled into a gravel parking area in front of an old weather-faded building. "You ever been to the pig races?"

She shook her head, more confused than ever. He escorted her into the restaurant.

"We'll have to come back on a weekend," he told her. "I think you'd enjoy them."

Pierce guided her to the back of the restaurant where, to her surprise, live pigs milled around in an enclosure beyond a short oval track a few feet below the level of the viewing gallery where they stood.

A gold statue—of a pig rather than a horse—and pots of black-eyed Susans completed the weird sensation of being at the races. Pierce watched in amusement as she stared at the setup then laughed in delight.

He explained the state had passed a law allowing this one place to have pari-mutuel wagering on weekends during the summer, the proceeds of which went to scholarship funds for high school students.

Shortly after, he seated her at their table, his glances warm in the dimness of the rustic building that could have served as a mess hall for local coal miners a hundred years ago.

"I feel like Alice when she went through the looking glass," she said. "Nothing seems quite real." She tried to smile but gave up when her lips trembled.

"What do you want to be real?"

She shrugged, helpless to come up with an answer, except the haunting yearning she couldn't name.

Chapter Nine

Chelsea went with Pierce to the Martel funeral on Thursday afternoon. The entire community was there. On Friday, she stayed at the cabin and read.

Alone that afternoon, she sat on the deck by the lake and pondered Pierce's ridiculous statement on Tuesday about his heart being broken. He'd been teasing, of course, but the words were ominous, a foretelling of what was to come. She knew who was in danger here.

If she didn't watch herself, she would fall in love with him all over again. That would be foolish in the extreme on her part. Making love only complicated the situation. To that end, she'd tried to send him home at night. He'd graciously but stubbornly returned to the sofa, refusing to give up the guard duty.

She checked her watch. It was nearly time for him to arrive. The heavy thud of her heart told her how much she looked forward to the end of the workday.

Pierce amused her with stories of the town and its denizens while they prepared a meal on the grill. They argued over television shows, watched movies and ate popcorn or ice cream as a bedtime snack, then went to their separate beds.

He hadn't argued about that when she'd insisted she wanted no further involvement. "It's your call," he'd said, giving her a little bow. She hadn't been able to read his expression.

One more week. All she had to do was hold out for one more week, then she would go home and put this vacation behind her, no better or worse for her stay in paradise.

Paradise?

She shook her head at the wistful description. A wise woman kept her feet firmly on terra firma. Hearing a call, she glanced over her shoulder.

Pierce was home.

He'd changed from his business clothes to shorts and a T-shirt. His hair, sun-streaked into attractive shades of light and dark, blew across his forehead as the wind swept down the valley, bringing relief from the terrible heat.

"Kelly wants us to come over tonight for supper. You game?" he called out as he drew near.

"I'm not sure I can get out of the chair. I've lounged here all afternoon," she confessed.

He bounded on the deck and, bending, tickled her bare foot until she burst into laughter.

"I'll go. I'll go," she said, fending him off. "Shall I change clothes?"

His gaze swept over her shorts and casual top, leaving a heated path in its wake. "No, you look fine." He offered his hand and helped her out of the comfortable deck chair.

"I found something in town for Kelly today. I'll give it to her now." She retrieved her purse and the gift she'd spotted at the store. "Okay, I'm ready."

They drove the few miles to the ranch in a friendly silence. She realized it didn't matter if they talked or not. The pleasure was in being together.

Frowning, she tried to decide if this was good or not. They arrived at the ranch house before an answer came to her. Kelly met them at the front door.

"Hi, you two. Chelsea, come on, I want your opinion on something. Jim's on the deck," she told her brother.

Chelsea followed her friend into a back room of the house. The room was newly painted in bright primary yellow.

"Look at this border," Kelly said, holding a roll of wallpaper next to the yellow on the bottom part of a wall. "What do you think? Is it okay in case the baby's a boy?"

Chelsea studied the print. It showed a lawn with toys scattered about it—a red wagon, balls of various sizes and colors, a yellow tractor with a rag doll on it—and a picket fence in the distance. "I think it's perfect."

"So do I. Jim wasn't sure about the doll and the fence, but what do men know?" she demanded with a laugh.

"Right. Here…I couldn't resist when I saw this at the store." She gave the gift to Kelly.

"Oh, how cute!" Kelly exclaimed when Chelsea urged her to open it. "It goes with the colors in here. Oh, and a mobile, too."

The gift was a wall hanging of red, blue, green and yellow balloons, each made of cloth, padded and quilted to make it three-dimensional. The mobile, to hang over the crib, was also balloons. When wound up, the mobile turned around and around and played a circus tune.

"Thank you." Kelly gave her a hug, then added, "You'd better get busy if our kids are going to grow up together."

"Don't hold your breath," Chelsea warned her friend, smiling at Kelly's meaningful grin.

Kelly thought she and Pierce were a twosome again. It was easier to let her believe what she wished than to argue about it. Kelly could be as stubborn as her older brother when she made up her mind.

They discussed the baby's room a bit longer, then went to join the men. Pierce hooked an arm around her in a casual manner while the other two consulted on the meal. He gave her a smile, his gaze lingering on her lips for an instant before he offered her a drink from his glass of iced tea.

She shook her head, then changed her mind and took a sip. Kelly gave her a nod of approval and announced dinner was served. They played bridge until eleven, then said their farewells.

"You were quiet tonight," Pierce remarked when they arrived at the cabin. "Something bothering you?"

"Not at all." Going inside, she put her purse on the counter next to the kitchen phone, then paused as she gazed at the calendar hanging there.

She flipped the page to the previous month, then frowned as she turned back to July.

"Counting the days until you go home?" Pierce asked, startling her as he stopped directly behind her.

She managed a laugh. "Of course not. Who wants a vacation to end?"

He leaned his head close to hers. "A woman usually has a reason when she studies the calendar so intently," he said in a deeper tone. "Do you?"

Fragments of thought flew around in her mind like a field of startled robins as she shook her head. She needed to think, to be alone. She spun around, intending to escape.

His hands settled on the counter at each side of her. "You have anything you'd like to share, such as worries about the future?"

"No." Her voice came out a reedy croak.

"Would you keep it from me if you were pregnant?" His eyes locked with hers as he waited for an answer.

She tried to maintain her defenses against his probing gaze, but finally she had to look down. "This is a ridiculous conversation."

"Are you late?" he asked quietly.

Heat flooded her chest, climbed rapidly up her neck and set her face afire. "No. Not really."

"If there's a child, I want to know."

She laid her hands against his chest as he moved closer. "There isn't."

His eyes narrowed dangerously, causing her insides to flutter in alarm. However, his touch was gentle as he slid his hands into her hair and lifted her face so he could see her expression clearly.

"You want a baby. Would it be so bad if it were mine?" he inquired with a hint of humor and more than a bit of sexy intent in his gaze.

"You said you wouldn't father a baby out of wedlock," she reminded him.

He studied her another moment, his thumbs rubbing soothingly over her hot cheeks. "Is that the only part you don't like—the thought of marriage?"

"I wouldn't force anyone into it," she said stoically.

His smile surprised her. "You modern women," he chided. He kissed her then.

Before she could recount all the reasons this shouldn't happen, her arms went around him as he pulled her close. Her lips opened to his, and she kissed him back with all the longing that had been building since the last time they'd touched this way.

Seconds, minutes, an eternity ticked by as time ceased to have meaning. If only an instant could be forever...

He lifted his head and studied her when they had to come up for air. "It's been this way from the first, hasn't it? From the moment Kelly introduced us, the awareness was there. It still is. Doesn't that tell us something?"

She shook her head. "What?" she asked defiantly when he frowned at her as if she were a slow student.

He laid a hand on her abdomen, his fingers spread wide, creating warmth deep within. "That's what we need to figure out. Maybe we should consider a trial engagement."

Shocked laughter rose and strangled in her throat. Tears burned behind her eyes. "I only have a week."

"Billings is barely an hour away," he countered, making it clear distance wasn't a problem.

Turning her back to him, she tried to think. The page on the calendar shifted restlessly as the breeze stirred through the cabin. She crossed her arms at her waist and wondered if she could possibly be with child.

He laid his arms over hers, his cheek at her temple. "I think we'd better consider marriage, Chelsea."

A tremor ran over her. "Why?"

"Just a hunch, but I think we've already made that baby you so desperately want."

"That's…that's just impossible. My doctor said it was highly unlikely."

But something in her countered that it wasn't.

He planted kisses along her temple, then turned her around with hands on her shoulders so that she nestled in his arms. "Is it?" he demanded.

"Fate wouldn't be so cruel," she said miserably.

Every muscle in his arms and along his back contracted into iron bands. Too late she realized the words had been thoughtless and totally rejecting of him in the role of father to her child.

He let her go. "Maybe not. Then again, maybe it would," he said with a sardonic half smile and walked out of the cabin, disappearing into the night.

She suppressed the urge to go after him, to explain she hadn't meant it the way it sounded, that she hadn't meant to hurt him. An equal need to weep or to scream assailed her. Why couldn't things stay simple?

Staring at the calendar, she wondered what she should do if there was a child. Unlike the reclusive librarian's lover, Pierce seemed determined to claim his place as the father. This from the man who had once declared he'd never intended a lasting relationship, at least not with her.

Which seemed less than ideal circumstances to begin a marriage.

A tremor shook her to her very soul. Marriage? The whole idea was scary. Look at what happened to her parents. She'd never subject a child to the unhappiness of her own youth as her parents grew to hate each other.

Pierce sat in his home office and stared out the window instead of working. Saturday was usually a productive day when he went over his own business accounts instead of doing the town's never-ending chores. However, other matters preyed on his mind today.

Mainly Chelsea.

Recalling their separation eight years earlier, he wondered if he hadn't been too quick to call it quits.

At twenty-eight, he'd been more of a hothead than he was at thirty-six. He'd wanted to cover the emotions that had cut through him when she'd said she'd been accepted in the forensic pathology program and it had hit him that she was talking about leaving. New York had seemed a world away from Montana.

Maybe they could have worked things out if he'd given them a chance instead of reacting out of hurt pride.

In truth, it had never occurred to him that she would go. Taken by surprise, he'd said the first thing that came to mind, mainly that he hadn't considered theirs a long-term relationship. He'd wished her luck and left her tiny apartment without a backward glance.

He'd had to leave, he admitted ruefully. No one liked to see a grown man cry. Instead of grief, he'd let the anger consume him. She'd chosen her career over him. Okay, he could live with that...and without her.

It had been damned hard, though.

At any rate, it would probably have been impossible to maintain the relationship. Her training had been out of state and far away. His business interests were demanding and would have kept him in Montana.

But maybe they could have worked it out. If they'd both wanted it. She certainly hadn't argued with him when he'd told her goodbye and walked out, but then, what woman would have? Chelsea had her share of pride, too.

Bah, he was crazy to be thinking such things. It was all water over the dam.

However, if she was pregnant, he wasn't going to stand by and do nothing. He had as large a stake in the future of the child as she did, so she could just get used to him being around. Billings wasn't far away, not far at all.

Restless, he made his weekly calls to the resort managers, then headed outside. A quick jog around the lake would clear his brain.

As he bounded along the trail, he spotted Chelsea sitting on the deck, a book in her lap as usual. He wondered how the lust and danger story was coming along.

Farther along, he spotted a man in a boat, a fishing rod in his hand as he waited for a bite. The man nodded cautiously to him.

Pierce smiled and waved at the resort guest he'd nearly drowned. A curious tightness entered his chest, as if his heart had enlarged and was squeezing his lungs. Her safety, her future, the possibility of a child, all were causes for concern. No one had ever worried him like this.

After circling the lake, he stopped at the deck and joined her. She closed the book and laid it aside. He saw it was a different book, a nonfiction one about solving cases using forensic evidence.

"Looks like interesting reading," he commented.

She nodded. "It deals with actual cases and the clues that led the investigators to the culprits. That helps keep my mind alert to the possibilities."

"Any ideas on Harriet's killer?"

"No, sorry. The trail is growing cold on that one. Unless someone knew who she was involved with."

"Let's go over there."

"To her house?"

"Yes. I've never been inside."

She cast him a doubtful glance.

"I need to shower and change. We can stop by her place, then go to lunch. There's a rooftop café in town. I don't think you've been there, have you?"

"No. That sounds interesting." She rose and took her book inside while he went to his house to get ready. When he came outside, she was waiting on his deck.

The sun picked up the auburn highlights in her hair while the breeze brought him the scent of her cologne. She'd changed to khaki slacks and a blue shirt. In wedge sandals that made her look taller than the five-seven he knew her to be, she was all slender curves and sweet womanhood.

"Let's go," he said, unable to conceal the huskiness of his tone as desire drummed through him.

At the Martel house, he detected a slight hesitation in Chelsea when they stepped over the police tape, which was broken, and entered the empty cottage.

"The door isn't locked," he observed.

"It never seems to be."

He felt a shiver run through her.

She paused and wrapped her arms across her middle. "Have you noticed the way closed, empty houses seem to become cold when no one lives in them anymore?"

He nodded. "It's as if they need people to breathe warmth into them."

"Yes."

"Tell me what you look for when you first enter a crime scene," he requested, looking around.

"If possible, you start at the outermost perimeter and work in toward the place where it happened. That way you aren't as likely to disturb or contaminate the evidence." She gestured toward the chair. "I wish I could have been here from the first. Too many people had been in and out by the time I viewed the scene."

"Do you think the sheriff and his men missed something? A small-town department probably seems inept compared to what you're used to."

"Not at all. I didn't mean to imply anything like that. Holt is very conscientious about his job."

Pierce frowned as emotion, which he immediately recognized as jealousy, darted through him. "You seem to get on well with the deputy."

"Yes—" She stopped and peered at him. "Are you implying something about him and me now?"

He smiled, knowing no one stood between them. "I know you better than that," he said softly, as if ghosts might be listening. The silence of the house was spooky. "The passion you shared with me hasn't been given to anyone else."

She opened her mouth as if to deny it, then set her lips together in a thin line.

He reached over and ran a finger across them. "When you do that, it makes me want to kiss you until your lips are soft again."

Her eyes flashed a warning.

He gestured toward the living room. "From the report, Molly came over from the library Monday morning and found her boss in that chair. How long had Harriet been dead?"

"I didn't examine her until Tuesday. She'd been in cold storage at the morgue for over twenty-four hours by then. The doctor there estimated she'd been shot sometime between Saturday midnight and dawn on Sunday."

"What do you think?" he asked, more curious about her mind and how it worked than in the actual answer.

Before answering, she walked over to the chair and stared at it, her manner concentrated and intro-spective.

"It's been unusually hot this summer," she finally said. "I checked the temperatures in the area that weekend. The thermometer hit nearly a hundred both days. That could make a difference."

"How much of a difference?" he asked, frowning at the idea of misinterpretation of the evidence.

"Maybe twelve hours. She could have been shot Sunday night."

"That was the night of the lunar eclipse. The town was full of people. The cottage isn't that far away from the city park. Why didn't anyone hear it?"

"With a celebration going on, a shot from a twenty-two probably wouldn't have been noticed at all." She pointed to a throw pillow on another chair. "The perp could have muffled the shot through one of those, then taken it with him when he left. I noticed the matching chair doesn't have a matching pillow."

"Is that unusual?"

"I would have to know the victim to know that. We'd better ask Colby about it. Or his mother. She'd be more likely to know. Could we go out to her house?"

Pierce saw that her mind was completely occupied with this idea. For a second he resented being closed out, then he realized his mother and sister complained of the very same thing in him when he was tussling with some decision for which there was no clear-cut answer.

"Sure. Right after lunch. We have reservations."

He smiled at the impatience evident in her eyes. Another trait they shared. He, too, liked to get right with it when he had a task to complete.

Giving in, he said, "Get the cell phone. We'll call and see if Louise is home."

"I can ask her now."

She dug the phone he'd given her out of her purse while he checked for a number in a directory they found in the kitchen drawer nearest the wall phone. Harriet had been a very organized woman.

He leaned against the counter and watched Chelsea do her job, admiring the kindness in her tone and the delicacy of her questions as she talked to Harriet's sister. He also liked looking at her.

"Louise thinks there were matching pillows," Chelsea said, excitement in her eyes for a second as she punched the off button on the cell phone. Her expression became somber. "Unless we can find it and unless it has evidence strong enough to pinpoint someone, we're no farther along."

"Any little bit might help," he said.

"True. I need to see Holt. Is he working today?"

Pierce saw his plans for a quiet lunch at the rooftop café vanishing. "I don't know. Call the sheriff's department."

She didn't have to look up the number. After she asked for Holt, she glanced at Pierce and shook her head, then spoke into the phone again. "No, no message. Thank you." She hung up. "He's off today. The dispatcher saw him in town earlier, so he's probably not at home."

"Leave a message on his voice mail and give him the cell phone number. Maybe he can join us for lunch."

"Good idea." She punched the redial button.

Pierce smiled wryly at the renewed enthusiasm in her voice. Had he not known it was his arms that she couldn't resist, he might have been tempted to sock the deputy.

After parking on Main Street, he guided Chelsea through the more formal dining room and up to the rooftop café, where several locals nodded and spoke to them as they were seated. The hostess left menus and cool glasses of water on the table before departing.

"Gossip central," he murmured, taking the chair beside Chelsea rather than across the table.

She looked around, forcing several people to quickly glance elsewhere or be caught staring. Pierce chuckled as she wrinkled her nose, then grinned.

"Let's give them something to talk about," she suggested, her eyes sparkling with impish intent. She raised her water glass as if in a salute to him, then took a drink, her gaze never leaving his face.

He did the same.

The humor faded as his eyes locked with hers. He delved into the verdant depths and wondered what she was thinking that made them go darker, as dark as a mossy pool found far away in a hidden forest.

His heart lurched drunkenly, banging off his rib cage as it beat hard and fast. The moment was interrupted by the arrival of Holt Tanner.

"Dispatch said you were looking for me," the deputy said, joining them. He leaned close to Chelsea and gave her a questioning stare. "I hope you've solved the case."

She shook her head, then explained in a quiet voice that didn't carry, her theory about the missing pillow, assuming there was one.

"Huh, we sure didn't think of that," the lawman admitted. His grin was weary. "I don't go around noticing whether stuff matches or not."

"That's why women are better at forensics than you guys are," she said loftily, bringing a lighter note to the seriousness of the discussion.

"You gals are just nosier."

"More observant," she corrected.

Pierce stayed silent and took in the interactions between the other two. Professional respect was obvious as well as friendship. Chelsea and the lawman were at ease with each other. While he had also shared such moments with her, most of their interactions had been spiced by the acute awareness they had for each other.

It came to him that he had no need to be jealous of another man, not while they shared this driving hunger that could only be appeased with each other.

Like a punch in the gut, it hit him that he didn't want her to disappear again the way she had long ago. There were things to be worked out between them. This time he wouldn't let her walk out of his life, not without a fight. It promised to be an interesting situation.

Holt glanced up from the menu the hostess had provided. "What's so funny, Your Honor?" he quizzed.

"Not a thing, Officer," Pierce said. He glanced at Chelsea, a smile tugging at his mouth. "Not a thing."

Chapter Ten

"I've got to stop by the office a minute," Pierce said when they were on the street once more. "Want to come up?"

"I think I'll stroll through the park. It looks cool under those cottonwoods."

"Okay, I'll meet you at that bench over there between the playground and the lake." He strolled off.

Chelsea entered the city park where a large number of the residents had gathered to escape the heat. Most homes didn't have air-conditioning and usually didn't need it, so the locals sweltered when the weather did one of these inversion things, as explained on the news last night.

She strolled along a mulched path, heading for the grove of cottonwoods near the lake. The lake was fed by an underground spring, which wasn't as large as

Cave Springs that supplied the water for the lake at Pierce's resort.

A deep sigh escaped her. He had carved out a good life for himself here in this friendly little town. He had his mom and sister, a brother-in-law he liked and a niece or nephew on the way. His house was lovely—

She realized where that train of thought was taking her and broke it off. It was none of her concern why he'd built a four-bedroom house in an ideal spot. Obviously, he liked his space.

Thinking of her own tiny apartment in Billings, she sighed again, unhappy without being able to say why.

The grove of cottonwood trees was quiet and shady, blocking out the heat and the shrill voices of some kids hanging upside down on the monkey bars. She followed a barely discernible path and found an outcropping of huge boulders forming a shallow slope of maybe five feet in height.

The temperature in this shady grotto was at least ten degrees cooler than outside. Water bubbled from beneath and around the stones, cascaded down the shallow drop and rushed into the lake with an impressive flow.

Delighted at discovering the source of the lake, she sat on a boulder and dipped her hand into the crystalline springs. The water was icy cold. With a laugh, she withdrew her hand and simply sat there, enjoying the moment.

The water sang a merry tune as it darted here and there around the rocky crevices. An occasional shout from the playground penetrated the thick canopy of leaves. A slight breeze rustled the shiny leaves.

She spotted a jay sitting on a limb, watching her with its plumed head cocked to one side, its gaze unblinking. After a bit, feeling ridiculously uneasy, she picked up a pebble and tossed it at the tree. The bird flew away.

Good. She didn't like being stared at. Smiling as if she'd routed an enemy, she turned back to the spring. In one clear spot, she could see her face as she bent over the water. It was like looking through a magic glass into another world and a different version of herself, one she didn't know. She was curious about that person.

A sheen of light outlined her head like a halo. A saint she wasn't, she reflected wryly.

Soft rustlings at her back brought her head around. Expecting the nosy jay, she found nothing stirring. Even the breeze had stopped, and the leaves hung motionless on the cottonwoods.

A chill invaded her, as if she'd swallowed an ice cube and it lodged in her stomach. A sense of impending…danger? disaster?…wafted around her like the icy remains of a spirit long departed.

She shivered, then stood, her eyes darting along the path, over the trees, catching at shadows, then moving again. With three easy jumps, she leaped over the burbling water and through the woods until she came upon the open field where several ball teams were at practice.

Relieved to be in sight of other people, she strolled across the lawn and around the lake until she reached the bench where she was to meet Pierce.

Sitting there in the sun, she felt the icy discomfort fade into drowsy warmth. Whatever had disturbed her so profoundly was gone now, its evil influence retracting to an unknown hidden place.

"Chelsea," a male voice called out.

Holt Tanner stopped in front of the bench. A young woman was with him. Dressed in a floral skirt and a purple silk blouse with a squash-blossom silver belt over it, she looked sort of New Age. She had long, wavy black hair and really beautiful gray eyes. Early twenties, probably. Petite in stature. Familiar.

"Hello, Dr. Kearns," the woman said.

"Please, call me Chelsea," she said. A light came on in her brain. "You're Tessa Madison, aren't you?"

"Yes. We worked together one time. In Chicago."

"I remember." Chelsea stuck out her hand. "I'm glad to see you again."

The young woman shook hands with her. A surprised expression came over her, then she shook her head slightly.

"What?" Chelsea said, sensing an undertone.

"Nothing," Tessa murmured and stepped back.

"Are you on the case?" Chelsea asked.

"Oh, no. I was walking through the park, on my

way back to the store, when I thought I recognized you. I knew you were in town due to the newspaper report."

Chelsea glanced at Holt, wondering why he was with the psychic.

"Pierce asked me to tell you he would be a bit late, if I saw you," Holt said, explaining his presence. "I saw you from the street when I was going to the cruiser and came over."

"I see. Have you met Tessa Madison?"

"No. How do you do?" he said politely but with obvious impatience. "I've got to be going."

"Thanks for the message," Chelsea said to his retreating back. She smiled at Tessa and moved over. "Join me? It's lovely here in the park."

"I've got to get back to the store and relieve my helper," Tessa said, but she sat down on the end of the bench, rather like someone waiting for the "ready-set-go" signal to start a race.

Chelsea laid a hand on the psychic's arm and felt her stiffen. "Tell me," she requested, drawing back.

Tessa looked unhappy. "No one knew about my abilities—or peculiarities, if you prefer—until you came to town. I didn't *want* anyone to know. Now everyone does."

"I did mention it. I'm sorry. I didn't know it was a secret. I thought you might be able to help. I sensed a…a coldness around the chair where the librarian died."

Tessa clenched her hands together, her face closed but troubled. "Death is always difficult."

"Yes. I felt something earlier, down by the spring, as if there was danger close by. Did you feel it when you touched me?"

"I...no. It was something else."

"What?" Chelsea asked, continuing her probe.

The lovely eyes, the color of rain, met hers briefly before Tessa looked away. "Congratulations on the coming little one," she said very softly.

Chelsea's breath hung in her throat and refused to come in or go out. Finally she swallowed and managed to breathe again. "So there is a child."

Tessa stood. "I'm sorry if it isn't what you want. I could be wrong—"

"No," Chelsea said in a husky croak. "I do want the baby. I'm very glad. Thank you for confirming it."

"Yes, well, goodbye, Dr. Kearns." She hurried off with a rustle of silk, leaving a faint fragrance of rosemary and lavender. A few feet away she turned and said, "You're not in danger at present, but you could be if you keep digging around. Everyone involved in the case could be in danger."

Chelsea watched the other woman until she disappeared from sight, her mind running in a thousand different directions and getting nowhere fast.

"Hey, beautiful," she heard Pierce call out.

Shading her eyes with a hand, she returned his smile and watched as he came toward her. His stride was long and easy, the step of a man confident in his world, a man used to taking responsibility, who would never dream of shirking his duty, as he saw it.

Including his duty to her and the baby.

Her breath hung up again and she had to force herself to breathe steadily and keep smiling.

"Wasn't that one of our local shopkeepers?" he asked, stopping beside her and dropping to the bench.

"Yes. Tessa Madison."

"The herbal place. I remember." He gave her a curious glance. "She seems rather quiet, but tense. Trouble?"

"Actually, no. She said we weren't in danger from the killer—"

"What!"

"But only as long as we don't keep poking around."

"Explain that," he demanded.

Chelsea hesitated, then said, "I've worked with Tessa before. She's a psychic. Sometimes she knows things."

Pierce snorted, openly skeptical.

"The killer is watching, but he isn't worried. He doesn't think he'll be caught. He thinks he's too smart for the rest of us."

She knew she was right as soon as she said the words. While she didn't get visions or anything like that, she sometimes felt things, call them hunches or intuition, and knew when something was right or wrong.

"Who is it?" Pierce demanded.

She shrugged. "That we don't know."

"That's the trouble with visions," he said cynically, relaxing against the bench once more. "Either they don't tell you enough to do any good, or they're full of detail, all of which turns out to be open to interpretation."

She smiled at his disgruntled manner. "Sorry, my crystal ball is in the shop." She stood. "Ready to go home? It's time for my nap by the lake."

He stood, his eyes darkening dangerously. "Yeah, mine, too," was all he said, although a devilish smile curved the corners of his mouth.

For a moment the need to tell him about the baby nearly overcame her reticence to divulge the news Tessa had told her. It was too early to know for sure. She brightened. She could get a pregnancy test kit at the grocery.

But not in Rumor. If Pierce heard about it, that's all he would need to send him off the deep end. He'd drag her off to the justice of the peace no matter what she said.

A shiver of excitement raced all the way to her toes. That didn't sound half-bad. And that fact worried her.

While Pierce attended to matters at the resort that afternoon, Chelsea finished reading through the forensic investigation book. Done, she sighed and examined all that she and Holt had discovered about Harriet Martel and the case of the missing lover.

Hmm, that sounded like a Perry Mason title. She wondered what the famed detective would have deduced from the clues in this case. What would he have noticed that she had overlooked?

This wasn't a stranger who had killed. Crimes of passion had roots that reflected a deeply involved relationship, one that had proved lethal to the reclusive librarian.

Laying the book aside, Chelsea got to her feet and paced the deck, her eyes on the cedar planks, her mind on the cottage where violence had erupted.

She could see the two figures, male and female, locked in a struggle for control, one demanding, one denying. She could hear their voices, the tone, not the words, as they quarreled. She could see the man pacing in fury.

Maybe he went into the kitchen, trying to collect himself, and Harriet used that moment to write the initials on the back of the book, using her own blood. She'd barely gotten the book replaced when he returned and demanded again that she get rid of the child. She refused. His fury exploded. He jerked open the drawer, grabbed the gun, swung it toward the infuriating woman and fired—

A crack of thunder broke into her thoughts.

Glancing westward, she saw dark clouds building rapidly around the peaks of the Beartooth Mountains.

A storm might bring some relief from the oppressive heat. Or it might trigger a forest fire, she corrected, seeing the flash of lightning in the distance.

Unbearably restless, she decided she'd take a walk now in case the valley did get some rain later.

"Chelsea, wait up," a familiar baritone called out when she reached the path encircling the lake.

She watched Pierce come toward her, a handsome man in casual clothes, self-assured, kind and hardworking.

"Going for a walk?" he asked.

"Yes. Join me?"

He nodded and fell into step beside her. They strolled along the path, their steps silent on the thick layer of pine straw that cushioned the trail.

He took her hand. "Thinking about the case?"

"Yes. It's maddening. There must be something we're overlooking, some simple fact that eludes us."

"Let it rest," he advised. "Sometimes things come to you when you least expect it."

"True." Strolling leisurely, Chelsea was intensely aware of their intertwined hands as they circled the lake. Her heart began a heavy warning beat that signaled danger. Huh, tell her something she didn't know.

They ran into other couples and families on the resort side of the lake. Most of the adults sat on benches in the deepening shadows of the pines while children, uncaring of the heat, played running games on the lawn.

Pierce chuckled. "Remember all the times we walked along the shore in Chicago, no matter what the weather?"

"Rain, hail, snow and sleet, we experienced everything Mother Nature could think of."

"Plus the wind. Montana blizzards were a breeze compared to Chicago winters."

"Then April came, and it was suddenly beautiful."

"Yes," he said. "April came."

April. The month she'd heard she been accepted in the forensic program. The month they'd parted. She watched the path and said nothing.

The lodge and cabins were left behind as they walked on. The cries of the children faded into the lazy trills of bird calls when they reached the wooded area.

"I'm sorry for what I said," he continued after a long silence. He glanced at her, then back at the trail. "That night I spoke out of hurt pride. You were so excited, so obviously glad to be leaving. I had to pretend it didn't bother me."

The hurt of that long-ago evening returned. The rumble of thunder reminded her of the storm that had blown in from the lake that distant night. The rain had fallen, but not her tears. Those had stayed inside, in her heart.

She tugged her hand from his and walked faster, as if that way she could escape the memories. "It was long ago. It doesn't matter."

"I hurt you. That matters," he said quietly.

"Why are you telling me this now?" she demanded, angry with herself because it still caused her pain. Only foolish people let the past continue to haunt them.

"To clear the air between us. I don't want the past overshadowing the present…or the future."

She started to tell him there was no future between them, but an inescapable truth asserted itself. If they had made a child, then their lives were indeed entangled.

The need to share her news rose in a painful gulp to her throat. "I think…"

The words wouldn't come. She tried, she honestly tried, but she wasn't ready to face the consequences of confession.

"I think it's going to rain," she ended miserably, coward that she was.

"You're right. I've felt a few sprinkles. We'd better make a dash for it."

A fresh wind swept down the mountain as they speeded up. It seemed to laugh at their efforts to outrun the storm.

Before they reached the cove and the narrow foot bridge that crossed it, lightning flashed brilliantly all around them and was immediately followed by a clap of thunder directly over their heads.

"Come on," Pierce shouted at her. He held out a hand.

Grabbing on, she ran all-out for the cabin set back from the lake. By the time they reached the porch, they were both drenched.

Shivers attacked her as soon as she stopped running. The rain changed to tiny balls of hail that pinged off the roof and skipped along the grass in a wild dance.

Laughing, Chelsea admitted, "I wanted a break in the heat, but I'm not sure this was what I'd envisioned."

Her companion didn't answer.

Glancing at him, she shivered again at the intensity of his gaze. Following it, she realized her cotton top had become transparent. Her nipples clearly stood out as dark circles beneath the wet bra. She crossed her arms.

"Too late," he murmured, a half smile touching his mouth and disappearing.

They stood there as if in a trance, their clothing dripping on the wood floor while the storm increased to a frenzied tempo. The hail changed to sleet. The wind grew icy cold, a foretaste of winter in its howl.

"We need to change." But she didn't move.

Neither did he.

It was as if they were frozen in time and place, cut off by the thunderstorm from all others of their kind. The isolation was complete, as if they'd been transported to an island far, far away.

His eyes went dark as he continued to gaze at her. She was aware of tension and hunger and the ache of unfulfilled yearning. Uncontrollable shivers raced over her.

He stroked her arms, then laughed. "I know a quick way to warm up." Spinning her about, he led the way into the house, closing the door against the wind once they were safely inside. Before she could think, he ushered her into the bathroom and flipped on the shower.

"Take off your clothes," he ordered. Without waiting, he stripped, in quick efficient motions, then looked at her. "Do you need help?"

She shook her head and edged toward the door before she could give in to the wild clamor inside her. "I'll let you go first."

He caught her before she could get away. "Let's go together," he suggested, his voice dropping to a husky note that vibrated along her nerves and drowned out any protests she might have made.

With his eyes never leaving hers, he began at her waist, unfastening the button and zipper and slowly easing the shorts over her hips.

"Pierce," she whispered.

He laid a finger over her lips. "Shh."

His smile took her by surprise. There was something plaintive, almost sad, in it that tugged at her heart. She opened her lips, inhaled deeply, but said nothing.

"I want to ravish you," he told her. "I want to kiss you until you melt in my arms, until neither of us knows where one stops and the other begins, until we're so lost in passion nothing else has meaning."

She made a little choking sound as the passion he spoke of rose to unbearable heights.

"That's the way it used to be," he said. "That's the way I want it again."

"This is insane," she managed to say.

"Yes, but it's the sweetest madness." He lifted the wet top over her head and tossed it aside. Her underclothes quickly followed.

Naked, he swept her into the shower, their bodies touching from chest to thighs to toes as the warm water sluiced over them, driving the chill from her bones.

His eyes dark with thoughts she couldn't read, he moved back enough to caress her with long strokes of his fingertips, his touch careful, as if she might disappear if he pushed too hard.

"I always thought you were the most beautiful woman I'd ever met," he told her, rubbing over her taut nipples with his thumbs. "That opinion hasn't changed."

She closed her eyes and laid her hands on his shoulders to steady a world that spun around her, wrapping her in a pink haze like cotton candy.

"Even when you were gone, I remembered how soft and smooth you felt," he continued, "how you responded when I touched you here…and here…"

He cupped her breasts with both palms, then slid his hands down to her waist and followed the line of her hips to her thighs.

"Look at me," he whispered.

Her eyelids were almost too heavy to open. Slowly she lifted them and met his gaze.

Grasping her hips, he skimmed his thumbs over her abdomen, probing gently. She felt a tightening deep inside, as if the developing child knew that touch and responded. When he dropped to his knees and planted rows of searing kisses over her torso, then ran his tongue around her navel, she went dizzy with sensation.

She moaned, then bit her lip to hold the sound in.

"Tell me," he encouraged hoarsely. "Tell me exactly what you want."

She thought of all the ways they'd ever touched each other. "Everything," she said. "I want everything."

He made a low sound in his throat to indicate his pleasure in her reply, then his touch became increasingly, tantalizingly intimate. Fire licked through her, and she grew weak with her need of him.

When she was ready to collapse, he released her and reached for the soap. With deft strokes, he spread lather over both of them, then rinsed them down with the spray attachment and flicked the water off.

In the silence she could hear the rain pelting the roof and windows. The storm outside continued.

"Come," he said.

He tossed her a towel before swiping another over his long, powerful length and used her blow dryer on his hair, then on hers when she was ready. She watched their reflections in the mirror, seeing them as two enchanted creatures in the mist. Her breath came quickly as she studied his perfect masculine form.

Cooler air swirled around them when he opened the door. She walked into the bedroom with him and stopped in the middle of the room while he turned down the bed.

He held out his hand. "I find I'm impatient for you," he said, his smile one of tender irony, as if he laughed at both of them and the hunger that drove them together.

"So am I," she admitted, and wrapped her arms around him so that she could experience the full sensation of his body touching hers.

He caught her hair in one fist and tipped her face up to his, his gaze locked on hers. "It'll be harder to get rid of me this time," he warned.

She hugged him fiercely, overflowing with passion and a jumble of emotions she couldn't identify. "I don't want to get rid of you."

"Then we understand each other." Bending, he kissed her chin, then her throat and finally the beaded tip of each breast.

"I can't think…when you do that," she told him, gasping as he became bolder.

He laid her on the bed, then stretched out beside her, his gaze roaming freely, leaving smoldering embers in its wake. Needing to touch him, she stroked down his chest to his hips, then bent forward, leaving her own trail of fire over his aroused flesh with ardent kisses and moist caresses designed to drive him wild.

When she became especially intimate, she heard his gasp of deep pleasure and felt his fingers entwine in her hair. Shifting, she pushed him against the pillows and leaned over him, delighting in giving him as much pleasure as possible.

"Enough," he said, and turned them so that she was against the sheets and he loomed over her, his eyes sexy and devilish as he caught both her hands in one of his and refused to let her free.

With a thousand demanding touches, he drove her crazy with need. The flames soared between them, but then he retreated, holding them to fleeting caresses until she bit at him in reckless defiance. He released her hands and let her in close again… and again…and again.

"This is as far as I can go," he said.

She thought he was going to leave. "No, no," she whispered, wrapping herself around him. "I want you. I want you now."

"My thoughts exactly," he assured her.

She sighed when he arched over her, merging them into one blissful whole. Shudders rolled over her, and the drumming of her heart drowned out the sounds of the wind and rain outside the cabin.

She felt his lips on hers, absorbing her cries as pleasure wafted in brilliant veils of color through her inner vision. "Pierce," she whispered desperately, needing him as she'd never let herself need anyone.

He answered her every desire, thrusting harder, deeper, until they were both sated with the wonder of all they shared. For a long time—she didn't know how long—they lay wrapped in each other's arms, neither willing to move as their hearts slowed and their bodies cooled.

At last he pulled the covers over them, and they lay side by side and watched the storm blow itself out, leaving a chill darkness in its wake.

Chelsea knew she'd made a terrible mistake. While letting him into her arms and sharing this wonderful magic, she'd forgotten to keep the door to her heart closed and locked. She'd fallen in love with him all over again.

Chapter Eleven

∽◎∽

The rain continued over the weekend, but by Monday the weather was fair and hot. Ninety-five degrees at noon, Chelsea noted on the digital display at the Whitehorn bank when she came out of the drugstore.

She opened the doors and let the car cool a bit before heading back to Rumor. She'd come over to do some shopping for toiletries…okay, the real reason had been to get the pregnancy test kit.

Now that she had it, she had to admit she was afraid to use it. She couldn't decide if she wanted the results to be positive or negative. She wanted the child, of course she did, but there was Pierce and his determination that they should marry if she was pregnant. Marriage was such an iffy proposition….

It was all too complicated to think about.

Arriving back in Rumor, she drove slowly down

Main Street. The town was busy at this time of day due to the lunch hour. She stopped behind a pickup and waited until the driver finished a conversation with a pedestrian, then moved on at ten miles per hour.

The shady deck by the lake would be the perfect place to wile away the afternoon. But first she'd stop by the diner and pick up something for lunch. Pierce had said he would be home late tonight due to a dinner meeting of the Chamber of Commerce, which was planning a to-do for September, so she'd have veggies and a snack for supper.

She stopped at the corner for a woman with a stroller to get across the street.

"Yo, Chelsea," a voice called.

She spotted Holt and rolled down the window.

"I need to see you," he said. "My office?"

Nodding, she turned the corner instead of continuing south to the cabin at the lake. After finding a parking space, she walked back to Main Street. The aroma of food coming from the diner was more than she could stand. She hurried in and ordered a sandwich and their largest container of iced tea with plenty of lemon.

"To go," she added, digging in her purse for her wallet. She wondered if Holt had eaten. "Make that two of everything," she told the waitress, "and throw in a couple of servings of the cherry cobbler. With ice cream."

The waitress laughed. "You're beginning to sound like me, Dr. Kearns. I stay hungry all the time. I'll be as big as a house before the baby gets here."

Chelsea smiled, not surprised that the waitress knew who she was, and willed the blush she could feel climbing her neck to go away. She was intensely aware of the pregnancy kit in her purse.

With lunch in hand, she hurried to Holt's office. He was hunched over the desk, eyes intent on the computer. He was wearing latex gloves, she noted.

"Hi. I brought food. Have you eaten?" she asked.

He glanced up in a distracted manner, then shook his head. "Haven't had time to think about it," he told her. "I've found something."

He made a space on the desk by lifting a bunch of folders and stacking them on another bunch, the whole looking like the leaning tower of Pisa. She set her burden down and straightened the stack.

"There," she said. "I won't have to worry about being crushed when that falls."

"Yeah, I've got to clean up the place pretty soon."

"Huh," was her skeptical comment. "Have you found something?"

"Yes, fingerprints, I think, but they aren't clear enough to dust." He pointed to the dust jacket of the novel from Harriet Martel's house, lying on his desk inside a plastic bag. "I've tried a computer scan, too, but that doesn't work."

"Have you tried super glue?"

He shot a questioning glance her way, stripped off the gloves and took the styrene lunch box she handed him. "Thanks. How do you use glue?"

She spread a napkin in her lap and picked up the chicken salad sandwich. "There's a method that sometimes works for latent prints. Let's eat and I'll show you."

He took a big bite, then peered at the sandwich. "This is good. I'd forgotten what real food tastes like. I've been living on peanuts, candy bars and coffee lately."

She "tsked" at him, then they wolfed down the entire lunch in fifteen minutes. "I'm ready for my nap," she said, wrapping the trash neatly and putting it in the bin beside his desk.

"You have to tell me about the glue first."

"We need a place to burn it. You have a lab table with a hood?"

"At the high school." He glanced at his watch. "If we hurry, we can get there before afternoon classes."

They took the book cover and glue across the street to the school, checked to make sure they could use the lab, then did the test. After burning a small amount of glue under the vent hood, a black haze appeared on the cover.

"By damn, these are fingerprints," Holt said, exulting in the discovery. "I just got a glimpse of something when I held the cover at an angle in the light. Let's go run them on the computer."

In his office, they photocopied, then scanned the prints into the computer. Chelsea studied the results, then shook her head. "There're two prints, probably an index and middle finger. They're smudged, though. There's only one well-defined area on one print. It might not be enough."

Holt wasn't discouraged. "We'll take what we can get." He started the computer check. "First the software will look at local records, then, on command, it'll run the prints against the FBI files."

He'd hardly gotten through explaining when the computer spit out a full report. By the disgusted look on the deputy's face, Chelsea knew their hopes were dashed. He whacked the computer keyboard with the heel of his fist.

"I don't see any point in running the FBI files. This isn't enough to be definitive." She indicated the print.

"Right."

"Maybe we'll find something else," she said by way of encouragement, although she doubted it.

"Well, sorry to bother you for nothing." He put all the prints in the Martel folder and tossed it on the desk. "I have to appear in court this afternoon. Someone's fighting a traffic ticket." He laughed with obvious sarcasm.

Chelsea said goodbye and left the building. A traffic ticket seemed so trite compared to a person's life…or someone getting away with murder. She was still pondering the unfairness of things when she reached the cabin.

After changing to shorts and T-shirt, she finished the new novel she'd started three days ago, then took a nap on the deck. Later she called her boss in Billings and reported on the findings there.

"We're at a dead end," she finished, "unless someone remembers something or we find another clue, which isn't likely at this date."

"You've done all you can. Try to enjoy your vacation," he advised.

"Right." After they hung up, she sighed, feeling nothing but gloom. "There is no joy in Rumor," she muttered, borrowing from a poem learned long ago in school. "The mighty Chelsea has struck out."

She had struck out professionally, and she'd struck out in her personal life. Her trip had been a waste of time.

Except for one thing. She laid a hand on her abdomen and opened a kitchen drawer with the other. The pregnancy kit nestled there with tea towels and a box of plastic bags.

Should she use it now? Or was it too soon to tell?

She was definitely late, but it was unlikely she was pregnant, no matter what vibes the psychic had felt at the park. The timing was off.

Unless she'd ovulated later than usual, a logical part of her argued.

All it would take was a three- or four-day delay, then a window of three or four days after ovulation for conception. That made a six- to eight-day difference, and the timing would work out just right.

She pressed a hand to her forehead. How could she have been so foolish? *Highly unlikely* didn't mean totally impossible. She had laughed at fate, and it had repaid her in kind.

Shoving the drawer closed, she decided to give it another few days. Until Friday. That would be two weeks from the time they'd first made love.

When Pierce arrived at nine, she was watching a movie, a huge bowl of popcorn in her lap. He'd stopped by his place, showered and changed to shorts and a T-shirt. His hair was still damp and smelled of balsam shampoo. He'd shaved, too.

"Umm," she said when he flopped on the sofa and nuzzled his face into her neck, "you smell good."

"You, too." He kissed her throat, then helped himself to the popcorn. "What are we watching?"

"Some horror movie about a mummy." She laughed when he made a face. "I love mystery and mayhem, don't you know?"

"Sadistic, that's what you are. You and Holt find out anything today?"

"Now why aren't I surprised that you know the deputy and I worked on the case?" she inquired innocently.

It was his turn to laugh. "Rumor is small but we aren't comatose. Let's see, you picked up two lunches at the Calico Diner, then went to his office. From there, you used the lab at the high school, then returned to his office."

"What, no mention of the romantic stop at the motel at the end of town?"

Pierce narrowed his eyes. "There is no motel in Rumor. And there better not have been any romantic stops anywhere."

"I'm not telling," she said loftily.

"Just for that..." He set the popcorn on the coffee table and proceeded to tickle her until she begged for mercy. "No mercy," he said, biting at her neck. "You haven't shown any for me."

"Ha!" she scoffed, then burst into laughter again as he dug wicked fingers into the sensitive spots just above her hipbones.

He nibbled at her tummy, then moved upward, a bit at a time, until finally their lips met and the laughter was silenced by sweet, potent kisses.

A long time later they came up for air and managed to catch the last thirty minutes of the movie. Pierce went to the kitchen to refill the glass of soda and get a beer for himself. The twist-off top wouldn't budge. He searched through the drawer next to the fridge for an opener. Not there. He checked the next one. Nope.

He started to close it, then stopped, his eyes widening as he took in the box almost hidden by the towels. He picked it up and saw it hadn't been opened.

Not yet.

When did she plan to use the pregnancy test kit? And did she plan to tell him the results?

He was pretty sure he knew the answer to that one. For a moment he could feel the blood surging in an angry tide through an artery in his neck, then he took a deep breath and carefully restored the kit to its hiding place.

There was no way he was going to let her leave town without a long, frank talk between them about the facts of life. He'd give her until the weekend to confess....

Friday arrived in the same sweltering fashion as the previous days. Pierce took the afternoon off. Chelsea loved it when he eased a canoe close to the deck and yelled an invitation for her to join him. They paddled about, exploring the lake, then later floated around in the swimming area on big rubber tubes.

"Let's see if Kelly and Jim feel like coming over tonight," he said when they left the tubes at the recreation room next to the lodge. "We'll grill some hamburgers at my place."

"Okay. I need to shower, then I'll come over and help." She looked at him in question.

"Grab some clothes. We'll shower at my place." He took her hand as they strolled along the path. "I'll show you my humble home. You haven't seen the inside yet."

After gathering slacks, blouse and underclothes, she went with Pierce to his cabin, which was at least twice as large as hers. She had to admit she was curious about it.

The deck extended beyond the roofed area, providing a natural extension to the living room. They'd eaten their Fourth of July picnic there, but she hadn't gone inside.

The front door opened into a foyer with natural stone floors that extended into a spacious kitchen and a powder room beyond it. The other floors were honey oak.

The living room was to the left and took up the entire western wall of the house, its windows opening to panoramic views of the hills and peaks beyond the resort. The dining area was separated from the kitchen by a counter and breakfast bar. Its windows looked to the north. Stairs along one wall lead to a loft and bedrooms up there.

"Here's the master bedroom," he said, leading the way to a room on the east side of the cabin.

His bed was king-size and covered with a blanket of Native American design in black, gray and burnt sienna. The frame was made of logs, and there were two matching chairs, plus a bench at the foot of the bed.

"The bath is through here."

Stone had been used for the floor, there, too. Double sinks had been installed in a granite countertop. A whirlpool tub occupied one wall. She could imagine relaxing in it and gazing out the windows into a meadow of wild flowers and the pine woods beyond that. In winter, it would be beautiful with snow—

"Shower or bath?" he asked.

She glanced at the shower tucked into a corner, then at the tub. Her answer must have shown in her face.

With a sexy smile he started the tub to filling, then added some aromatic herbs. "An old Indian remedy to restore vitality and peace of the soul."

Inhaling deeply, she detected mint and maybe wood violets in the mixture. When Pierce started to undress, she did, too, no longer self-conscious after a week of living with him.

"Get in," he invited.

When she did, he turned on the jets so the water bubbled and swirled around her, then climbed in with her. She found there were many delightful things an inventive couple could do in a relaxing bath.

Later, washed and dressed, they barely had time to start the evening meal before Kelly and Jim arrived with a fresh strawberry pie from the diner for dessert.

"I'm starved," Kelly announced, giving them each a hug. "Ah, good, you have the hamburgers on." She helped herself to sliced vegetables, assorted chips and dips.

Finally, noticing the others watching her, she peered at the carrot she was devouring, then back at them. "What?"

Chelsea and the two men laughed while Kelly tried to look indignant. Giving up, she laughed, too, and helped herself to three kinds of pickles, which she proceeded to eat with a generous serving of onion dip.

Pierce couldn't help wondering what Chelsea would be like during pregnancy. Would she eat everything in sight? Or would food make her nauseated?

He noticed how easily she worked in the kitchen and how naturally she took to the role of hostess in his home as she refilled the chip bowl and teased his sister about leaving something for the rest of them.

Contentment spread through him, coming not only from the passionate hour they'd spent in the bath, but also from this moment of sharing with his family. Chelsea fitted very nicely into the scene.

What would it take to convince her of that?

"Deep, dark thoughts, brother?" Kelly demanded.

"Not really. Just wondering what I ever did to deserve such an obnoxious younger sister."

"Honey, would you sock my brother?" she asked sweetly.

Jim held up both hands. "I'm not involved."

Kelly gave Chelsea a sly grin. "Chelsea, would you see if you can put him in his place?"

"Chelsea can wrap me around her little finger," Pierce announced grandly. "But sisters are a pain."

Kelly's eyes went wide. "Wow," she said softly, with loads of meaning.

He checked the meat, declared it done to perfection and piled the hamburgers on a platter Chelsea handed him. Their eyes met briefly. He noticed her smile, the graceful way she moved and the quietness that indicated she'd emotionally withdrawn from something that bothered her.

He leaned close and whispered, "Was it something I said?"

Startled, she stared at him, then surprised him by blushing. "I don't know what you mean."

"I'll tell you later," he promised.

"Hey, whispering in public isn't polite," Kelly complained, setting the plates and silverware on the patio table. "Oh, listen, music."

From over the water came the romantic sounds of a love song. "There's a dance at the lodge tonight," he told them. "The guests were getting restless in this heat, so the manager planned a dessert party with dancing under the stars tonight."

"Oh, let's go over," Kelly requested. "I love to dance, and we haven't been in ages."

Pierce felt Chelsea's reluctance in the remote way she smiled and kept silent. "Would you like that?" he asked.

After the briefest hesitation, she nodded.

"Okay," he said. "After we eat."

"Good idea," Kelly said. "I'm starved."

That brought a laugh from the other three, and Chelsea seemed happy and attentive the rest of the meal. He didn't question why that made him happy, too.

Shortly after nine they walked the short distance to the patio that was serving as the dance pavilion. When he ordered iced tea for Kelly and a pitcher of margueritas for the rest of them, Chelsea shook her head.

"I'd prefer iced tea," she said, quiet again.

"Lots of lemon," he added to the waiter.

The significance of the request wasn't lost on him. Had Chelsea used the kit and did she know she was pregnant? The need to know was driving him crazy. Had it been just the two of them, he'd have demanded an answer right then and there.

"If we're going to have fun, let's get at it," Jim quipped, standing and holding out a hand to his wife.

"Why don't men like dancing?" Chelsea asked, watching as the other couple joined the dancers.

Pierce took her to the floor and enfolded her in his arms, liking the way she felt when she was nestled against him. "It makes them self-conscious in front of other people," he said. "Sometimes it creates problems for our libidos that we can't control easily."

He grinned when she peered up at him. Her smile was automatic, but he could tell her thoughts were elsewhere.

On the coming child?

With an effort, he held the words in, biding his time until they were alone and could speak freely. For the next hour they talked and laughed and danced.

"Oh, I hate to leave, but I'll be dead on my feet tomorrow if I don't get to bed soon," Kelly complained in her good-natured way, pressing her hands to the small of her back. "Would you believe I have four possible deliveries this weekend?"

"The population is multiplying by leaps and bounds," Jim murmured, shaking his head as if at some unexplained phenomenon.

"It's the spring water," Kelly told them as they headed back to the house. She poked Chelsea in the ribs. "Are you drinking a lot more than usual?"

"Nope," Chelsea declared.

Pierce chuckled at the quickness of her answer, but he also saw her smile falter for an instant. The little clues and nuances he kept picking up, not to mention the test kit, intrigued him more and more. A discussion was definitely called for.

"Lightning up on the mountain," Kelly said. "Are we due for another storm, do you think? It brought a nice drop in the temperature the last time."

Jim agreed and added, "But not enough rain. That's what we really need. The forest is still as dry as tinder."

They stopped on the path and watched another zigzag of light streak across the peaks to the west. They heard the faint rumble from the first strike.

"Three miles away," Pierce said, having counted the seconds since the flash and the arrival of the thunder. "The sky is clear overhead. I doubt if we'll see any action out of those clouds."

At the house, after saying their farewells to his sister and brother-in-law, he caught Chelsea's hand. "My place or yours?"

"Wh-what?"

He wondered at the little catch in the word. "Shall we stay at my house or yours tonight?"

She stiffened for a second, then relaxed. "Mine. I'm used to it. And the ice cream is there."

"Do you have a sudden craving for pickles, too, like Kelly?" he asked in carefully casual tones.

The silence that followed arced between them like a fireball of electricity, static but crackling with untold danger and menace.

"Hardly," she said.

Her deprecating laughter didn't quite ring true. Tonight, he decided. Tonight she would tell him what was going on, or else they were in for a long session of truth seeking.

For a minute he wondered if she would lie to him. In spite of the sexual attraction, did she want him out of her *real* life?

"I'd like to talk," he said once they were inside the smaller cabin.

She turned on the television. "Let's see if we can catch any news about the storm."

He stifled his impatience. He had something he needed to check on before the confrontation. Leaving her pretending to be engrossed in the news, he went to the kitchen and looked for the test kit.

It had disappeared from the drawer. Every nerve in his body tightened, then relaxed. They were definitely going to have that talk. Tonight.

Quietly closing the drawer, he returned to the living room and settled on the sofa beside her. He liked the warmth of her body next to his. He liked the faint scent of her cologne and the way the hair grew at her temples, tempting him to kiss her there. He refrained.

Talk first, he reminded himself. He focused his attention on the news. A storm was headed their way. Not much rain was expected, nor much relief from the unusual heat, but the lightning was almost sure to spark more forest fires in the area.

Picking up the remote control, he hit the off button and the set went dark. "Now," he said, turning toward her.

She cast him an uneasy perusal. "Yes?"

"Have you used the pregnancy kit yet?" he asked.

A ripple of pure shock chased over her face. For a second, she looked as if she might faint or scream. Being Chelsea, she did neither.

"Tell me the truth," he requested in as quiet a voice as he could muster. He didn't want to frighten her or have her think he was angry. "Are we expecting a baby?"

Chapter Twelve

Chelsea opened her mouth, but no sound came out. She was, for the first time, truly speechless.

"Yes or no?" Pierce said. "It's a simple question."

"Really, Pierce—"

"Yes or no?"

She rose, then paced to the dark window and stood looking out as if admiring the scenery. Lightning danced along the clouds, which now stretched long cumulus fingers toward the town.

"Yes or no?" he said in a harder tone.

Turning, she faced her relentless lover and, her voice barely audible above the frantic thump of her heart, said, "I appear to be."

He sprang up as if hit by a lightning bolt. Ramming his hands into his pockets, he stopped in front of her. "Were you ever going to tell me?"

"Yes. I would have. When I was sure," she added at his doubting stare.

"Did you use the pregnancy kit?"

She gasped. The blood rushed to her head, making her dizzy and unsure. "How did you know about that? Were you snooping through my things?"

"No. I saw it in the kitchen drawer last night when I was looking for a bottle opener. It isn't there tonight. So the test was positive?"

"Yes."

"Is it accurate?"

"You can get a negative reading if you use it too soon, but if it shows positive, it's pretty much conclusive."

He clasped her upper arms and peered into her face, looking very solemn. "It isn't the end of the world," he said quite gently. "I'll help, you know. We'll share the cost and the responsibility."

"It isn't necessary."

His hands tightened, then relaxed. "It may surprise you women, but some men are interested in their offspring and want to take part in their lives." His smile was more than a little sardonic and a bit edgy.

"I'm sorry. I didn't mean to imply differently."

"Come," he urged, still gentle with her as he led the way to the sofa. Once they were seated, he said, "Marriage would be best in my book, but you seem violently opposed to the idea, so I guess that's out. Are you planning to nurse?"

She pressed a hand to her temple. He moved so fast, her mind couldn't keep up. "I haven't thought that far ahead." She considered. "Yes, I probably will."

"Then I'll come to your place on weekends, or you can come here. Later, when the baby is weaned, you won't have to bother. I can hire a baby-sitter to help during the summer."

She blinked, too stunned to respond as he calmly planned the future. It hurt that she didn't seem to have much of a role in those plans. Had she wanted him to insist on marriage?

A clap of thunder startled her to the point that she jumped. Wind swept through the windows like a demon on the prowl. Something in the bedroom fell with a noticeable thud.

Pierce frowned and released her. He closed all the windows and, in the bedroom, restored the clock on the bedside table. After making sure the house was secure, he came back to her.

"Don't worry," he said softly, smoothing the frown on her brow with one finger, "I won't interfere in your life any more than necessary and only where it concerns the child."

She stared at him helplessly, overcome by a sense of loss and sadness she couldn't fathom. Tears burned her eyes.

"Chelsea?"

"Thank you," she managed to whisper.

His expression changed to concern. "What bothers you?"

Pivoting, she walked a few steps away. "Everything seems terribly complicated right now. It's difficult to think what's best."

Silence throbbed between them, then she heard his footsteps behind her. He laid a hand on her shoulder.

"You accept me in your bed. Why is it so hard to give me a little space in your life?"

Again his tone was gentle, as if he dealt with an invalid. She gazed at him in despair. "A child takes up more than a little space. It will be lifetime commitment, one you didn't ask for."

"Neither did you."

"But I want it."

His eyebrows lifted. "So do I," he murmured, his eyes on her mouth. He bent his head. "So do I."

He kissed her then, and she clung to him as if, in his arms, all the troubles of the world could be solved. Knowing they couldn't, she hugged him harder and returned his kisses with a desperation that came from the heart. She wished this night would never end.

It would. All good things did. One more day, then Sunday she would go home.

Pierce lifted her into his arms. The phone rang. Bending, he let her pick it up and answer. "Hello?"

"Chelsea? This is Holt."

"Holt," she murmured for Pierce's benefit. He put his head next to hers and listened.

"You won't believe this, but guess who's arrived in town?" Holt demanded in disbelieving tones.

Chills dashed up her neck. "Who?"

"Warren Parrish."

The name didn't ring any bells. "Who's Warren Parrish?"

"Harriet Martel's estranged husband."

Chelsea woke with a start. Something was wrong. "Pierce," she said, giving him a shake. She threw the covers off. "Pierce, there's smoke in the house."

He was out of bed in a single bound. He slipped into his jeans and followed her through the house. "It's outside," he said when they reached the kitchen without finding a source of the fire.

Going onto the screened porch, they saw flames etched against the dark sky, licking skyward as they danced along the treetops. As they watched, a tree exploded with a *boom*. Embers burst from it like a gigantic shower of fireworks.

"Forest fire," he said. "The wind is driving it toward the town. Damnation." He spun and raced inside.

She did, too. The phone rang a few minutes later. Chelsea, sitting on the bed to put on her shoes, answered.

"Chelsea, this is Kelly. Several firefighters have been trapped behind the fire line. A rescue team has gone in to bring them out. I'm setting up a field hospital at the park. Can you help?"

"Of course."

"I need to talk to Pierce."

Chelsea turned the phone over to him. "Where's the fire line?" he asked.

"About three miles northwest of here," Kelly told him. "The wind is driving it toward the Stewart ranch. Jim's over at the fire station. The chief asked for you. I told him I'd give you the alert."

"Thanks. We'll be there in five minutes." He hung up and glanced at Chelsea. "Ready?"

"Yes."

They ran to his SUV and took off. Driving up Main Street, Chelsea could see the ominous red line of fire moving down the mountain toward the valley.

Pierce muttered a harsh expletive. "We need to call out the volunteers," he told her. "The whole town will have to help with this one." He stopped at the park. "There's Kelly. I'll see you later." He touched her arm. "Take care."

"You, too." On an impulse she didn't question, she leaned toward him. They kissed briefly but deeply. She leaped out and raced toward the library where Kelly directed operations for a field hospital. "What do you want me to do?" she asked, stopping beside her friend.

"You're here. Good." Kelly pointed behind them. "We're setting up an emergency first-aid station.

The hospital in Whitehorn is sending all the ambulances they can spare. The worst cases will be taken there. We're using the basement of the library as an infirmary. We'll assess damage and treat for smoke inhalation and minor burns. Can you carry these?"

Chelsea helped Kelly carry supplies from her car into the makeshift infirmary. Several cots were already set up along one wall. Partitioned off from the room by screens, an examining area was being prepared by several women. She recognized Pierce's mother, Mrs. Dalton, and Louise Holmes, stacking towels on a table.

"Everything is disinfected," Mrs. Dalton called out.

"Here," Kelly said, handing several surgical packs to Chelsea. "I'd rather do this at the office, but there's no place to put anyone when we finish."

Chelsea observed her friend with admiration. Kelly gave orders like a general, her manner calm, efficient and sure. "You seem to have done this previously," she commented, preparing a tray next to an examining table.

"A couple of times," Kelly admitted, laying out her own instruments at a second table. "Also, I've lived through several fires in the area. None has ever reached the town."

"I'm praying it won't this time. Knock on wood," Louise voiced the old superstition and knocked on her own head.

"There's always a first time," Kelly said, worry flashing through her eyes, then she was all brisk motion as she finished the setup and handed Chelsea a surgical gown.

Chelsea eyed the table as she fastened the gown. "Are we expecting other medical personnel?"

"Nope. We're it on the front line. The doctors in Whitehorn will be needed at the hospital. We'll mostly do screening and first aid."

"It's been a while since I did an emergency room rotation," she reminded her friend. It had probably been five years since she'd examined a living body.

Kelly glanced her way with an encouraging smile. "Don't worry. It'll come back to you. I'll be here if you want a second opinion."

A siren rent the air, the noise so loud it was impossible to speak for a minute.

"The emergency call for volunteers," Kelly told her. "Everyone is needed."

Thirty minutes later the local volunteers, Jim and Pierce among them, brought in the first victims of the fire. Six firefighters had been trapped by a crown fire while digging a fire line. Two of them were unconscious.

Chelsea knew a crown fire jumped from treetop to treetop and could create its own gale-force winds as it burned. It moved with terrifying speed. She pulled on gloves and bent over the man placed on her table.

While she automatically checked his vital signs, she noted how young he was. No more than twenty at the most. "Oxygen," she said.

Someone handed her the mask and turned on the tank. Her eyes met Pierce's. She smiled her thanks and clipped the mask into place, then peeled the soot-covered shirt open. His chest was red but not blistered. His pulse and blood pressure were good. His eyes responded to light. After a few breaths, he coughed and opened his eyes.

"Am I in heaven?" he asked, and gave her a cheeky grin.

"The library basement," Pierce informed him.

The men laughed while Chelsea continued the examination. She smoothed an antibiotic ointment on the reddened skin and dressed it. "Okay…rest, lots of water, aspirin for pain," she prescribed.

"Doc, we got a guy who needs help," a man called out. He led another young man into the examining area.

She winced when she saw his arm. His shirt was burned away and the skin was one giant blister from wrist to elbow. She peeled her gloves, pulled on a clean pair and picked up a scalpel. "Put him here," she ordered.

Pierce helped the firefighter onto the table. He held a basin per her instructions while she drained the blister, then covered it in a special burn cloth that would keep it sterile and help it heal. She gave the firefighter a shot to ease the pain. "Take him to one of the cots. He'll be asleep in a minute."

Pierce and the other man took the victim to the opposite side of the room. Mrs. Dalton appeared. "I'm trained in first aid. Who needs help?"

"Chelsea," Kelly answered from the next table, putting ointment on a burned hand. "My nurse is here with me."

Chelsea spotted the woman at Kelly's table. Mrs. Dalton stepped up, gave her a smile and waited for orders.

"Next," Chelsea said.

Before the next man could step up, two firemen brought in a third young man. Blood pumped steadily out of the injured person's leg near the ankle.

"What happened?" she asked.

"Slipped and cut himself with the fire ax," a fireman explained. "Looks bad."

"Lay him on the table," Chelsea said, changing gloves automatically. "Kelly, I think I'll need some assistance."

Kelly gave instructions to her nurse, then joined Chelsea. She reached for a sterile pack. "I'll administer the anesthetic. You do the repair. You were always better at that sort of thing than I was," she argued when Chelsea frowned and started to protest.

Chelsea reviewed what needed to be done, then concentrated on doing it to the best of her ability. She found her skills were intact. Her hands were steady, almost moving by instinct as she found the end of the artery and clamped it, then fished out the other end.

Together, as if they were back in medical school, the two woman worked to stem the loss of blood. With the artery no longer pumping blood into the wound, they cleaned the painful slit and bound it, making the patient ready for transportation. In a few minutes they signaled the medical attendants who were on standby.

With siren wailing in the smoky darkness, the driver and paramedic took the firefighter to the hospital in Whitehorn for a permanent repair.

Mrs. Dalton wiped down the table with disinfectant, put the used items in a covered metal bin and prepared for the next victim of the fire. Kelly and Chelsea stripped their gloves, slipped into fresh surgical gowns, sprayed disinfectant on their hands and arms, put on fresh gloves and were ready for business again at each table in less than two minutes.

Other people—male and female, smoke jumpers and volunteers—were brought to them. Dawn broke, but the smoke kept the sky dark. The fire burned steadily along the crest of a ridge, but the firefighters managed to keep it from roaring down upon the town.

At noon, a hand touched her shoulder. "Break time," Pierce murmured. "You need food." He let her finish with a bandage, then led her off.

Her assistant had changed a couple of times. The pregnant waitress was helping now. She shooed Chelsea off and cleaned the table and straightened the instrument tray. Chelsea had lost count of the number of wounds, mostly minor, she'd treated.

It wasn't until she sat down at a picnic table in the park that she realized how tired she was. Jim and

Kelly were already there. Two teenagers hurried over with box lunches from the Calico Café and asked what they would like to drink. The girls brought over large containers of iced tea.

Chelsea pulled thirstily on the straw. When she glanced up, she noticed the men's clothing was covered in soot. They'd washed their faces and hands, but the black was embedded around their nails and in the knuckles. They looked beat. Pierce had several small red places on one hand.

"What have you two been doing?" she asked.

"Trying to hold a position," Jim said. "We've been beating out stray fires that ignite behind the fire line. Embers are blowing everywhere."

"Are we winning or losing?" Kelly wanted to know.

"Winning. For now." Pierce opened his lunch box, noticed that Chelsea's was still closed and switched his box for hers. "Eat. You've been working for eight solid hours."

The aroma of corned beef tempted her appetite. She picked up a sandwich half. "It's like war, isn't it? I never realized, but fighting a fire is a battle."

"We'll win," Pierce told her. "We have to."

Their glances met and held. She saw the determination in him and the certainty of victory, also the knowledge that victory came with a price, a price the whole community would have to pay. He, as mayor, would bear the brunt of it, for he would have to encourage and comfort the residents through the disaster if they couldn't save the town.

She touched his cheek lightly. "We will," she murmured, needing to encourage and comfort him.

He caught her hand as she withdrew, and pressed a kiss into her palm. "Hold that thought," he said with a smile, and closed her fingers around the kiss.

Across the table Kelly looked on with approval.

Chelsea felt an incredible sense of oneness with them, these friends who made her feel needed and wanted. It was something she didn't recall ever experiencing in her whole life. It would be so hard to leave….

The rest period didn't last nearly long enough. Holt, as dirty as Pierce and Jim, ran into the park, stopped near their table and shouted, "We need all hands. The fire has breached the line. All hands, on the double."

The picnic area was emptied of all but women who had young children with them, older people and the teenage girls who started cleaning the vacated tables. Kelly grimaced and stood. "Ready?"

Chelsea nodded. They returned to the makeshift field hospital where Kelly's nurse and a retired practical nurse worked over some new patients. She and Kelly pitched in and helped finish up. After cleaning the area and restocking their supplies, they sat down and waited.

Two fire trucks from Whitehorn blasted into town. The fire chief directed them to the north side where the fire, visible to the whole town, burned steadily down the mountain. They could hear booms, like cannons going off, coming from the inferno.

She wondered where Pierce and Jim were, but didn't let herself dwell on their safety.

Holt stopped by and said they were evacuating families who lived between the fire and the town. One old man, a recluse who lived up in the woods, couldn't be found. His cabin had burned to the ground. Worry cut deep lines in the deputy's brow.

Kelly put some soothing salve on his face where tiny red burns indicated how close he'd been to the flying debris. Ash was now thick in the air, settling on hair and clothing like a shroud.

"Where do you think the guys are?" Kelly murmured after Holt bounded off again.

"In the thick of things."

Kelly sighed. "That's what I figured. Look, here comes our next patients."

Chelsea went outside to help unload the walking wounded. One of them was the fire chief's assistant. Blood oozed from a scalp wound where he'd been hit by a flying limb from an exploding tree.

"There'll be more," the fireman said. "The fire jumped again, trapping these men. A rescue party got all but one out. We're trying to clear an opening for the two who went in to rescue the guy we couldn't find."

"Who are the trapped men?" Kelly asked.

The fireman shrugged. "Could be anyone. We have more than a thousand men on the fire lines."

Chelsea and Kelly glanced at each other, then went to work on the new patients. For the rest of the afternoon they were on their feet, examining, making snap decisions, treating the injured or sending them to Whitehorn. When the Whitehorn hospital was full, the forest service chief called in helicopters and transported emergency cases to Billings.

A lull came at sunset. The sky turned an awesome red, backlighting the trees that still stood sentinel along the western horizon. To the north, the blaze dimmed, then flared, dimmed, then flared, as the firefighters won and lost ground during the long afternoon and evening.

Someone had brought in lawn chairs. Chelsea and the medical team sank wearily into them when the last patient was treated. "Are we winning?" Kelly asked, watching the fiery tongues lick the sky as the sun disappeared.

No one had an answer.

Chelsea wondered about the two men who had gone back to rescue another. Had they gotten the man and returned? Who were they? Meeting her friend's eyes, she knew Kelly was wondering the same thing.

At midnight the fire chief reported the fire was contained. A cheer went up from those who worked behind the lines, making sandwiches and coffee and tending to the weary warriors who stumbled back to town for rest and food, then headed out again to face the enemy.

By dawn there were pockets of heavy smoke but no evidence of flames on the hillside. Helicopters with water tanks dropped hoses into the lake, slurped up water and flew off to release it on the smoldering ruins of the forest.

"I wonder where the guys are," Kelly said as the sun came over the eastern hills.

Chelsea wondered, too. She and Kelly had slept on cots for a few hours, taking turns being on call. Chelsea recalled being awakened only once for a case that required stitches. A female firefighter had fallen and gashed her scalp on a rock. The young woman had returned to duty as soon as she was patched up.

"People show such remarkable courage when it's needed," she said. "We can be petty and mean, but we're good when it comes to emergencies."

Kelly nodded, her eyes on the northern horizon. "I don't feel good," she said.

Chelsea was on her feet at once. She'd worried about Kelly and the baby at spare moments. "Are you in pain? Are you having cramps or backaches?"

"I'm okay. I didn't mean me. I meant..." She stopped and inhaled deeply, slowly, as if she sought control.

"Jim and Pierce," Chelsea said, sinking into the chair once more. "I know. I'm worried, too. We haven't seen them in hours."

"Have you noticed how well they work together?" Kelly looked at her. "Just the way we did yesterday and last night. Rumor isn't large, but it and the county could support a family clinic—"

Chelsea held up her hand. "Please. I can't think right now. I'm too beat." She managed a smile.

Kelly smiled, too. "I know. That's why I thought I'd tackle you now, while you're too tired to argue. I think we'd make a wonderful team, you and I. Brenner and Dalton, the Montana miracle workers."

Chelsea tried to think this through. "Dalton?" she finally had to ask.

"You. You and Pierce will marry," her friend announced.

"Don't...don't make plans that will only end in disappointment," Chelsea advised, an ache settling deep inside her.

Kelly gave her a disapproving frown, but said nothing more as two grandmotherly women brought them plates of ham and eggs and fresh biscuits. "Mmm," she said, biting into one of the biscuits, "these are from the diner. They make the best hot breads and pastries of anyone."

Chelsea was almost too weary to pick up the fork. She got down a few bites, then set the food aside. Where was Jim? Where was Pierce?

Volunteers were streaming back into town, sharing hugs and kisses with their families and friends, telling of their close calls and encounters with the demon fire, their mood cheerful and relieved after the tension of the past twenty-four hours.

Chelsea checked her watch as she realized only a bit more than a full day had passed since she and Pierce had been awakened by the smoke.

A day. A lifetime.

"Where are they?" Kelly murmured, sipping from a steaming mug of coffee, her eyes on the horizon.

"They'll be here soon." Chelsea wondered if Kelly believed her. She didn't know if she believed herself. "They will," she insisted.

Two hours later a field truck pulled into the library parking lot. "Casualties," the forest service medic called out to them, as Chelsea and Kelly stood at the basement door.

"Oh, God," Kelly said. She rushed forward.

Chelsea grabbed her arm. "They'll need us here."

Two stretchers were brought in. Jim and Pierce lay on them, their bodies limp and unconscious, their faces so blackened they were almost unrecognizable. Oxygen tubes were clipped to their nostrils.

"They crawled into a hole under a boulder," one of the medics explained. "I don't think they're injured, but the smoke nearly got them."

"I'll handle it," Chelsea said. "You sit down."

Kelly, her eyes stricken, shook her head. "I'll help."

But Chelsea, after a quick checkup, knew the signs weren't good. Kelly didn't need to be attending her husband or her brother if…if…

No, no, no, her heart cried.

"Let's get them to Billings," Chelsea said. "Are the helicopters back yet?"

"Not yet," the nurse reported. "I'll call."

A long ten minutes passed. The two men breathed in shallow gasps, the sound loud in the silent infirmary. A medical evacuation chopper arrived.

"Come on," Chelsea said to her friend. "Everything's done here. We'll go with them."

The two men were strapped onto the stretchers mounted on the landing gear while the two women rode inside with the pilot. Chelsea called in a report to the emergency medical staff who waited in Billings. The EMT swung into action as soon as they arrived.

Resuscitators were hooked up to relieve the stress on the men's bodies. A precise mix of oxygen and air flowed into their lungs. Medicine administered through the steady drip of fluid into their veins stimulated the uneven heartbeats, which soon smoothed out into regular spikes on the heart rate monitors. Their rooms were side by side in the critical care unit, per Kelly's request.

The nurses gave Kelly sympathetic glances as they went about their duties, having learned the firefighters were her husband and her brother.

Chelsea told the nurses she was a friend and was asked to wait in the ICU waiting room.

"No," Kelly said fiercely. "She's to stay. My brother would want her to stay."

No more was said about sending Chelsea out. Mrs. Dalton arrived an hour later, and the three women waited together, moving from room to room, always making sure someone stayed with each man. Shortly after lunch the men were moved to twin beds in a semiprivate room.

At one point Pierce muttered darkly. "Chelsea," he said over and over. "Chelsea."

She stood beside the bed and took his hand. "I'm here," she whispered, bending close.

"Stay," he said, briefly opening his eyes.

"I will," she promised.

Sometime late in the afternoon, Mrs. Dalton took Chelsea's hand. "Thank you for being here. Pierce needs you, not just at this moment, but in his life. Tell him you want to be married as soon as possible."

Chelsea was stunned. "It isn't as simple as that."

Mrs. Dalton sighed. "You young people make everything so difficult," she murmured, but her smile was kind.

Chelsea thought about marriage. She swallowed hard. Maybe it was time she and Pierce had a real heart-to-heart talk. The thought frightened her almost as much as the fire had.

Chapter Thirteen

Sunday evening Pierce and Jim were awake and restless. Other than a cough that would last for days, if not weeks, while their lungs cleared of inhaled soot, they felt fine and demanded to know when they could go home. When the doctor who had treated them stopped by, that was the first question the two patients put to him.

"Your vital signs are strong," the physician noted, studying the charts. "You can go in the morning."

"Why not now?" Pierce demanded.

"Tomorrow." The doctor, who recognized Chelsea, spoke to her. "The main concern is a buildup of fluid in the lungs and pneumonia. That will need to be watched for a few days. However, they're strong and healthy, so I don't expect a problem. Other than stubbornness," he added, smiling.

Chelsea nodded.

"No running, lifting or other strain on the lungs," he gave instructions to the patients. "You'll be coughing a lot. If it interferes too much with your sleep, I can prescribe something, but I'd rather let nature do its job without interference if possible. You'll have sore throats for several days. Don't talk."

Chelsea nodded toward Kelly. "Kelly is also a physician. Between the two of us, we can handle them."

"Right," Pierce said, which produced a laugh. "With two doctors to watch out for us, we'll be okay."

After a brief discussion, the doctor signed the release forms and went on about his rounds. Chelsea cleared her throat. Everyone looked at her. "My apartment is only a few blocks from here. Everyone is welcome to stay there tonight, then we can rent a car to get us back to Rumor tomorrow."

"I have my car here," Mrs. Dalton reminded them.

"Great," Pierce said, his voice so hoarse it hurt to hear him speak. "Let's stay at Chelsea's, then head back to Rumor in the morning."

Kelly also thought that sounded fine.

By eight, the five were ensconced in Chelsea's apartment. She gave Kelly and Jim the tiny guest bedroom and put Mrs. Dalton in her room. She settled Pierce on the sofa in the den, which was also her office. She would sleep on the love seat in the living room, which was rarely used.

After supplying nightgowns and T-shirts for the others, she showered, put on fresh clothing and decided to run to the store for milk, bread and eggs to serve for breakfast. She called her favorite pizzeria and ordered two large pizzas and asked to have them delivered.

When she returned from the store, the pizzas had arrived. They gathered in the den to eat and watch the news. They wanted to make sure the forest fire was still out.

Chelsea, observing the others, realized this was the first time she'd had guests at her place.

"Your apartment is darling," Kelly told her after the news and weather report were finished.

"Very comfortable," Mrs. Dalton chimed in.

"Let me know what you think in the morning," Chelsea said with a smile. "My bed is ancient. It's left over from college days." Her glance was apologetic.

"I'm sure it's fine," Mrs. Dalton said. "You know, a place in the city would be nice for shopping trips and visits. You could even live here and commute to Rumor. If necessary."

As four pairs of eyes gazed at her, Chelsea felt a blush rising and tried to forestall it by the power of suggestion. It didn't work.

Jim covered a yawn and told them he was ready to try his bed out. He and Kelly said good-night and left them.

Chelsea heard him coughing as he and Kelly went down the short hall. Mrs. Dalton gave her son a kiss on the cheek and went to her assigned room.

Chelsea shut the door to the den so Pierce could have privacy and went to the kitchen to put their plates, glasses and utensils in the dishwasher. She prepared a pot of coffee for breakfast and set the brewing timer for six o'clock. She knew Pierce was an early riser.

"Thanks for having us over," Pierce said, coming into the kitchen. He cleared his throat, coughed harshly and settled on a stool at the breakfast bar.

"It's a pleasure." She wiped the counter and tossed the paper towel in the trash. "You're my first guests."

"Do you know many people here?"

"Not many." She glanced at the clock. "I need to call the police chief and let him know I won't be on duty tomorrow. I thought I'd ride down to Rumor with you so I can pack, then come home in my car."

Pierce nodded and stood. "Stay with me tonight," he invited. "I'm sure I'll sleep better."

She glanced down the hallway, then back at him.

"My mother won't mind," he said dryly.

"It isn't that." She thought of what Mrs. Dalton had told her—to simply tell him they were getting married. She couldn't do that, but she wanted to reopen the topic for discussion. But words wouldn't come.

Pierce went to the den. Pausing, he bade her good-night, then he went inside.

Chelsea felt the emptiness when the door closed. She turned out the light and stood in the dark. Down the hall, she heard Kelly and Jim in the bathroom, then Mrs. Dalton, as they prepared for bed. Finally all was quiet.

Still she stood there. Her legs ached, and she realized just how tired she was, how tired they all must be. She took a step, paused, then took another.

Quickly, without letting herself think, she opened the door to the den and slipped inside. Pierce stood at a window, gazing out at the lights of the town. He wore briefs and the T-shirt she'd given him. He smiled upon seeing her.

"Good," was all he said, then he slipped between the covers of the sofa bed and folded the sheet neatly across his chest.

Chelsea brushed her teeth, put on pajamas and returned to the den in record time. When she slipped into bed beside him, he turned off the light and pulled her close.

Then he coughed. And coughed.

An hour later he turned on the light. "Maybe I should go to another room so you can get some sleep."

"You'll be more comfortable in the chair." She pointed to the big easy chair next to the end table. She got a light blanket from the closet. "You'll be able to sleep better sitting up while your lungs clear."

"I won't be able to hold you," he complained.

She smiled at his plaintive tone. "It's a chair and a half."

He looked interested. "What does that mean?"

"Sit. I'll show you."

When he was settled, she folded the bed into a sofa again, then sat beside him in the oversize recliner. After spreading the blanket over them, she pulled the lever which brought the footrest up and let the chair recline. With a weary sigh, she snuggled against him.

Wrapping an arm about her, he murmured, "I like this."

It came to her that this might be the last time they were together. Grief squeezed her heart into an aching knot. She would live through it. She had eight years ago.

"Will you let me sleep with you when I come to see the baby?" he asked, his cheek resting on her head.

"That wouldn't be wise," she said.

His arm tightened. "Probably not," he said.

He sounded oddly quiet, almost sad. But then, she might be reading her own emotions instead of his. Never had she felt so discouraged by life, not even when he'd told her he hadn't wanted a lasting relationship with her.

Tell him you want to be married.

Not tonight. Maybe when he recovered. Or when

she felt stronger and able to handle rejection. Right now she was terribly tired. Tomorrow she'd be okay.

She sighed against his warmth, feeling his strength surround her. Tomorrow she'd also be alone again.

Monday, Pierce listened while Chelsea called the police chief and told him all that had happened over the weekend. It pleased him when her boss told her to take the week off for rest and recuperation before returning to the office.

"You can stay at the cabin," Pierce said.

He noticed she didn't answer. Okay, he hadn't expected handsprings, but she didn't have to look so damn sad. It troubled him, that look in her eyes, the remote smile that said she wasn't really there.

After she locked the apartment, they joined the others in the compact car, he and Chelsea in the back, Jim and Kelly riding in front with his mom.

Pierce thought his brother-in-law looked weary. He knew he was. Both had coughed frequently during the night, making it hard for everyone to sleep. Coughing was good. It made it less likely either would get pneumonia or other infections, according to Kelly.

Once in Rumor, Pierce asked Chelsea to drive the SUV while Kelly took charge of getting Jim home. Mrs. Dalton hugged both men. "Rest," she admonished. She gaze earnestly at her son. "Follow your heart," she said softly.

He nodded. His heart led to Chelsea, but that was a dead-end road. She'd trampled his idea of marriage into dust when he'd brought up the subject.

At his house Chelsea made sure he was comfortable on the sofa with lots of pillows for support. She even laid an afghan at hand in case he got cold. He didn't point out the temperature was in the eighties and it wasn't even noon. A haze of smoke lingered in the air.

"Will you be okay while I go next door?" she asked.

"Sure. But hurry back."

She gave him a worried perusal before leaving. He settled into the corner of the sofa, content to be an invalid at the moment. As soon as he could take a deep breath without coughing and his lungs stopped burning, he would take advantage of her concern.

For the next hour he channel surfed and imagined various scenarios in which those advantages could play themselves out. It was a pleasant interlude. He even managed to catch a short nap.

After he woke, though, he grew restless. Where was Chelsea? He'd assumed she'd be back soon.

Finally he rose and went to the deck. From there he had a clear view across the creek to her cabin. He was just in time. She put a suitcase and the bag containing her laptop computer into the trunk of the car, then went back into the cabin.

With a muttered curse, he headed across the grass at a jog. Before reaching the creek, he was racked by coughs so violent he had to stop and bend forward to get his breath.

"Pierce, what are you doing?" Chelsea demanded. She dashed across the stepping stones and grabbed his arm. "Are you crazy? You're not supposed to run. Get inside."

"Your place," he insisted when she tried to turn him.

Shaking her head in exasperation, she held his arm as if she thought he might pass out at any moment. At her house, she pushed him onto the sofa, then got him a glass of iced tea with a generous squirt of lemon and a spoonful of honey.

"The lemon will help clear your throat," she advised, hovering around him.

He caught her hand and pulled her down beside him. "Were you going to sneak off without saying goodbye?" he demanded, furious with her and life and everything else that crossed his path.

"Sneak off?" she repeated. "Why would I sneak off?"

"Beats me. If you want to go back to Billings, I won't try to stop you. I probably couldn't, anyway," he added. He realized it wasn't his call. It was up to her.

"I'm not going back, at least I hadn't planned to for a few days. Unless you'd rather I did."

"You put your stuff in your car."

"Oh, that." She touched his shoulder as if to comfort him. "I was going to bring everything over to your place. I thought you'd be more comfortable there. I was cleaning up the cabin so you could rent it."

He searched her eyes for confirmation. She was telling the truth. Relief speared through him. He cleared his throat, coughed, sipped the tea, then took her hand. "I have some things to tell you," he said. "Will you listen?"

Chelsea's heart beat very fast as she nodded. When he moved over, she sat on the edge of the sofa, her hip pressing lightly against his while she waited for him to speak.

"Thanks for taking care of me," he began.

Disappointment was so sharp she nearly wept. "I didn't do anything. I mean, it was part of my job."

He shook his head. "Will you let me finish?"

She nodded. She knew what was coming. She'd been through this goodbye once before.

"I don't know how to reach you. I guess I never did, but I'm through hiding how I feel."

Startled, she could only stare at him.

"I think we could have a good life, either here or in Billings. The commute wouldn't be all that far."

His voice became raspier as he spoke. He sipped some tea while she clenched her hands and tried to quell the painful temptation of hope that swelled in her.

"Together?" she asked, not sure what he was saying.

"Yes."

"For...for the baby?"

"Of course. But for us, too." He reached up and caressed her cheek, leaving a burning sensation everywhere he touched. "We've shared friendship and passion. I think it's time for more."

In spite of her attempts at calm, bubbles seemed to be forming in her blood, effervescing into her brain so that she couldn't think. "More of what?" she asked, her voice almost as raspy as his.

He inhaled deeply, shot her an apologetic glance as he had to cough, then spoke. "We were in love eight years ago," he said softly. "I think we still are. At least, I know how I feel. I want you to stay with me...always."

The bubbles inside her frothed like shaken champagne. They danced through her mind, a golden dust sprinkled into her dreams by laughing fairies. "Pierce," she whispered.

"Marry me, Chelsea," he said, "and let's find the life we were meant to share."

She opened her mouth, but no sound came out. Finally she buried her face against his neck while tears filled her throat.

"Is that a yes?" he asked, his manner tender as he cradled her in his arms.

"Yes," she managed to whisper in a croaky voice. However, the last haunting remembrances of the past remained. "But are you sure this is what you want, or is it pressure from Kelly and your mother?" She looked at him anxiously, seeking the truth.

He looked surprised, then he frowned fiercely. "No one can force either of us into a marriage we don't want. This is strictly between us. I do love you, you know."

"You didn't want a lasting relationship before."

"You surprised me when you told me about the residency. I realized you were talking about leaving. It hurt, and I reacted out of pride. Can you forgive me?"

Staring into his eyes, she saw truth and gentleness, a warmth she realized was for her...*her*. "Yes."

"I didn't give you a chance to explain," he continued. "I promise to listen in the future. If I forget, you can hit me with a two-by-four to get my attention."

At his smile, she smiled, too. Inside, an ache pressed against her rib cage, but it was a good ache, one of love and hope and all the things that would be their future.

"I love you, too," she said. "I have since we first met. Why was it so hard to say before?"

He nuzzled his face against her hair and kissed along her temple. "We both had some growing up to do. We also had some baggage from the past—your parents' divorce, which made it harder for you to trust, and the death of my father, which made the loss of a loved one harder for me to handle. Let's promise to always share our fears and doubts."

"Always," she said solemnly.

Their eyes met and held. His love flowed over her like a warm blanket of peace, woven with passion and tears and joy and a great deal of love.

"How soon can we be married?" he demanded.

"I'll call my folks and see how soon they can come. How about a small wedding here by the lake?"

He nodded. "Let's close up the cabin and head over to my place…our place," he corrected.

When they arrived at the house, the phone was ringing. Chelsea answered while Pierce coughed from the exertion of walking from the car to the house. "Hello?"

"Are you two going to marry?" Kelly demanded.

"It's Kelly. She wants to know if we're going to marry," Chelsea told Pierce.

He grinned and held out his hand. Chelsea gave him the phone and snuggled into his arms on the long sofa. "Yes, my nosy sister, Chelsea and I have decided on marriage." He held the phone away from his ear while she shrieked like an banshee and yelled the news to Jim.

"Do I get to be matron of honor?" she finally calmed down enough to ask.

He looked at Chelsea, who nodded. "Yes, but only if you're extra nice to me for a whole year."

Kelly was immediately indignant. "You're surely not waiting a year to marry, are you?"

Pierce glanced at the woman in his arms, the woman he'd loved from the moment they'd met. "No, we're surely not," he said and kissed her, briefly but with feeling.

"Good. I'll call Mom and tell her, although she won't be surprised."

"Is she psychic?" he asked, mildly curious. Actually he was much more interested in exploring the smoldering passion he could see in Chelsea's eyes.

"I guess. She said last night that it wouldn't be long before you two woke up. She wants *all* her grandchildren to be legitimate. Are you two expecting?"

A faint flush hit his face as he realized everyone in his family seemed to know about him and Chelsea. With a laugh he relaxed and confessed all. "We think so."

He felt Chelsea's laughter as he waited out another series of shrieks. A smile tugged at his lips. "Come over for dinner. You and Chelsea can discuss symptoms then. In the meantime, don't call us—we'll call you." He hung up.

Chelsea gazed into his eyes. Little tremors began to stir deep inside her. "You're injured," she reminded him.

"Deep breathing is good for clearing the lungs," he told her. He found the spot on her neck where she liked to be kissed and proceeded to do so.

"You're not to strain—"

"I won't," he interrupted her protest. He stroked the smooth skin under her knit top until he had to have more. Cupping her breast, he murmured, "You can do all the work this time," he told her.

Chelsea relaxed. "Okay, this is Anatomy 101," she teased softly, pushing him into a reclining position.

He pulled her head down to steal a kiss. "I love you," he whispered.

"I love you," she replied, and remembered something one of her professors had said a long time ago when she was starting her medical training.

"Love," her professor had said, "is the best medicine of all."

It was. It truly was.

* * * * *

SPECIAL EDITION

Life, Love and Family

THE TEXANS ARE COMING!

Reader-favorite miniseries Montana Mavericks
is back in Special Edition with new loves,
adventures and more.

July 2011 features *USA TODAY* bestselling author
CHRISTINE RIMMER
with
RESISTING MR. TALL, DARK & TEXAN.

A Texas oil mogul arrives in Thunder Canyon on
business and soon falls for his personal assistant. Only
one problem—she's just resigned to open a bakery!
Can he convince her to stay on—as his bride?

Find out in July!

Look for a new
Montana Mavericks: The Texans Are Coming title
in each of these months

August	September	October
November	December	

Available wherever books are sold.

www.Harlequin.com

SEMM0711

SPECIAL EDITION

Life, Love and Family

LOVE CAN BE FOUND IN THE MOST UNLIKELY PLACES, ESPECIALLY WHEN YOU'RE NOT LOOKING FOR IT...

Failed marriages, broken families and disappointment. Cecilia and Brandon have both been unlucky in love and life and are ripe for an intervention. Good thing Brandon's mother happens to stumble upon this matchmaking project. But will Brandon be able to open his eyes and get away from his busy career to see that all he needs is right there in front of him?

FIND OUT IN

WHAT THE SINGLE DAD WANTS...

BY *USA TODAY* BESTSELLING AUTHOR

MARIE FERRARELLA

AVAILABLE IN JUNE 2011
WHEREVER BOOKS ARE SOLD.

Finding Her Dad

Janice Kay Johnson

Jonathan Brenner was busy running for
office as county sheriff. The last thing on
his mind was parenthood...that is, until
a resourceful, awkward teenage girl shows
up claiming to be his daughter!

*Available June
wherever books are sold.*

HARLEQUIN® HISTORICAL:
Where love is timeless

USA TODAY BESTSELLING AUTHOR
CAROLYN DAVIDSON
INTRODUCES HER
WILD WESTERN HISTORICAL

Saving Grace

SHE IS FIGHTING FOR HER LIFE...
BUT THEIR LOVE CAN HEAL ANYTHING

If ever Grace Benson needs a man to ride to her rescue,
now is the time—and Simon Grafton is the man! When he
encounters her being brutally attacked on the roadside by her
uncle's farmhand, Simon doesn't flinch. He'll risk anything to
defend this innocent from a madman still on the loose.

As Simon helps her heal and gain a new foothold in life,
it becomes clear that his heart is what needs defending.
Soon, his only course of action is to make her his bride....

Available from Harlequin® Historical
June 2011